It was a friendly vi
Now they're up ⌐

PEARL SKY

It's not just any holiday season in the immortal world. Elder Zhang's oldest servant is reaching the century mark, and Ben and Tenzin are ready to celebrate, but no sooner do they land on Penglai Island than a mystery falls in their path. A valuable seal has gone missing, and the artifact was a gift from an ancient vampire who just happens to be heading to Penglai for a long-overdue formal visit.

The Elders of Penglai may have asked Ben and Tenzin's assistance to find the lost treasure, but that doesn't mean that eight ancient vampires, their immortal children, and all the humans who serve them will suddenly become open books. Penglai Island is secret for a reason, and the heart of that reason may just reveal the motive behind the theft.

PEARL SKY is a brand new Elemental Legacy story by Elizabeth Hunter, ten-time USA Today bestselling author of the Elemental Mysteries, the Irin Chronicles, and other works of fiction.

Praise for Elizabeth Hunter

Do not skip this book! It sets up for so much more of [Ben and Tenzin] in the future. I had no idea of the potential these two had and I AM HERE FOR IT!

— This Literary Life

I think one of the things I love most about these characters is their banter back and forth - Ben does love to tease Tenzin - and this book definitely hits on those notes.

— Courtney, Goodreads reviewer

...As with any Ben and Tenzin book, the surface plot is richly interwoven with an exploration of larger themes: concepts of change, growth, justice, and forgiveness, among others.

— Kathryn, Goodreads reviewer

Pearl Sky

An Elemental Legacy Story

Elizabeth Hunter

Chapter One

They would know. How could they not know?

They were the wisdom of the ancient world; immortal warriors, scholars, and kings.

Nearly gods.

They would know, but he had no choice.

Fate had anointed this for him, though the act might—probably would—end in his death. Fate had given him one task to accomplish in his short, fleeting life. One gift he could give to the world, one song that must be heard.

She must be heard.

He was the only one, the only one who saw her dimming light. Unless he did this, she would die as he would, an insignificant human living an insignificant life. And he knew —he *knew*—she was destined for more.

The man stared at the golden seal before him. The luminous black pearl glowed with an inner fire, staring back at him from the dragon's eye. Swirling milky-white-and-golden-brown jade surrounded the glowing dragon; intricately carved carp swam among lotus flowers and churning waves.

It was a priceless treasure.

No.

Everything had a price. Everything.

The man took a delicate hammer and chisel to the wood around the seal and methodically began to tap.

Chapter Two

B en woke at dusk, the dark scent of his mate filling his senses. She surrounded him, her simmering amnis snapping in the air like electricity before a storm. Before he opened his eyes, he reached for her, and as their skin met, the spark snapped, then dissolved in the damp air of the river house.

"Did you sleep?" He kept his voice a whisper.

"A few minutes."

He knew she usually slept longer but wasn't surprised that her layers of armor hadn't allowed her to dream. They were hours away from Penglai Island, formal seat of the Eight Immortals and home of their sire, Zhang Guolao.

They had arrived at the river house the night before, their last stop on the flight from the West Coast. They were going to Penglai for a celebration, but his mate was not in a celebratory mood.

He smelled the river that ran through the courtyard, the moss covering ancient stones, and the familiar aroma of bone broth simmering in the outdoor kitchen of their house in the water town east of Shanghai.

She moved over him, burrowing her face into the crook of his neck and filling her nose with his scent. He smiled because he knew what she smelled there, their joined blood and amnis mingling until he could barely distinguish one from the other.

To Ben, his mate's blood smelled of heady spices, honey, and cold winter air. She was Tenzin, ancient daughter of the northern steppe, commander of immortal armies, heir of an ancient king, and legendary vampire assassin.

She was also his mate, the woman who made him question his sanity nightly, and the most frustrating, maddening, and addictive vampire in existence.

"I want to have sex." She sat up, straddling his hips. "Why are your eyes still closed? You're not sleeping anymore."

"I'm enjoying all my other senses." His body was awake and his erection was pressed between them. He reached out and felt for her hips. She was naked from the waist down, but he felt the edge of a thin chemise fluttering against her skin. "This is nice. Silk?"

"Yes." She shifted her hips, rubbing her body against his. "You're being lazy."

"No." He kept his eyes closed, sliding his fingers up and taking the chemise with them. "I'm taking my time."

She could be an impatient monster when it came to carnal appetites, and Ben loved to torment her. He played his fingers over her skin, the gentle rise of her breasts, the sensitive flesh of her inner arm, the slight curve of her belly. His fingers drifted down to the apex of her thighs and she shivered, surging forward until his fingers grazed her sex.

"No." He laughed and pulled his fingers away, flicking his tongue to taste the hint of her before he gripped her hips and rolled them over, bracing himself over her and finally opening his eyes a second before he entered her body.

"Hello, mate." He smiled at her expression.

Her eyes were clouded with pleasure, her mouth was open, and the edge of her fangs had nicked her lower lip.

Ben thrust his hips forward as he bent down and captured her blood, licking the spicy salt of it and sucking her lower lip into his mouth. He swallowed her groan and gripped a handful of her hair at the nape.

She wrapped her legs around him and pulled him deeper. Ben froze at the heady sensation of their bodies joined. He released her mouth and pressed his forehead to hers, their breath mingling as their bodies moved as one.

When they were joined like this, he couldn't measure time. Moments were counted in breaths and tremors. Minutes passed with the flow of blood and pleasure that sparked beneath their skin like the immortal current of energy that kept them alive.

Sometimes her pleasure crested in a wave he eagerly followed, and other times his climax battered him with the force of a hurricane and she would chase it, forcing him to come again until she could match his pleasure with hers.

That night her climax rolled through her, lifting her chest as she flung her arms around his neck, pulled his throat to her mouth, and bit.

Pleasure blasted through his body, and he gave in to the

pull of her lips on his skin and her fangs in his body as he found his release.

Take it. Take it all. If she killed him in that moment, it would be a fair death.

"I love you." He breathed the words into the frenzied air around them. A canvas clapped against one wall, and the wooden shutters in the library slammed shut. Two wind vampires lost in the throes of sexual passion tended to create interior windstorms.

Tenzin pulled away after she sealed the wound on his neck. "I thought we secured everything after last time."

"Must have missed a couple of things." He rolled to his back and pulled Tenzin to drape over his body, running his fingertips over her back and watching the tiny hairs along her skin rise to his amnis everywhere he touched.

She murmured something in her mother tongue, and Ben forced himself to stay silent. He was slowly picking up a word here and there, mostly from studying modern Mongolian and other Altaic languages. He'd understand more after their two weeks in Penglai since Tenzin and Zhang usually argued in it when they wanted secrecy; they were the only two surviving speakers.

Or were they?

It had been months since the strange fire vampire in New Orleans had mentioned a name that froze Tenzin in a way he'd never seen before.

Temur.

The blood of Temur remembers who you were.

Ben didn't know if Tenzin realized he'd heard the strange Russian vampire shout the phrase. He hadn't asked her about it, but he'd felt the spike in her amnis and the ensuing violence of her furious wind.

The blood of Temur.

She'd been restless and moody since they'd returned from New Orleans, and now they were headed to one of Tenzin's least favorite places in the world—her father's fortress island temple, Penglai.

The past wasn't past. In that moment, it was very much the present.

———

BEN AND TENZIN LANDED IN THE INTERIOR COURTYARD of Zhang's compound on the island, the living quarters of each elder determined by territory and element, though each was given the same amount of space to signify their equality in political status.

Officially, each elder held the same level of influence and power. Unofficially, Zhang was the founding member of the council, the oldest, and could have easily been the leader, though he happily handed that honor to his longtime ally Lu Dongbin, a water vampire of similar age and sensibilities as Zhang.

As they'd descended over the golden-lit jewel of an island in the eastern Bohai Sea, Ben had noticed an unusual number of wind vampires patrolling the skies.

Once their feet touched ground, they were immediately greeted by Tai, Zhang's head of house, and Gan, their sire's head of guard.

Tai, an elegant vampire with shoulder-length black hair,

refined Han features, and a quiet nature, was well-known to both Ben and Tenzin.

Gan was new to the island, a Mongolian vampire recently promoted from Zhang's territory in Khentii. She was tall and broad with high cheekbones and a defined jaw that reminded Ben of their sparring sessions with Gan's favorite weapon, the battle-ax.

Both vampires bowed deeply as their elder's children landed in Zhang's home, and Ben and Tenzin bowed in return.

Tenzin must have picked up on the unusual tension too. "What's happened?"

Gan quickly said, "I'll let Tai fill you in." She nodded to Tenzin and Ben. "It's good to see you both, but I need to return to the guardhouse. I'll meet with you later if you wish."

"Sounds good." Ben frowned and turned to Tai. "I thought we were coming for a party."

"Erdun's party is still happening." Tai motioned for them to follow him out of the courtyard and into a hallway. "Let's get some tea."

"Is Zhang in danger?" Tenzin asked.

"Absolutely not," Tai said. "Neither are any of the elders. What's happened has political consequences perhaps, but it will all be sorted out."

Ben and Tenzin exchanged glances. "Was someone hurt?" Ben asked. "Is that why there's all this extra security?"

The Eight Immortals of Penglai Island were the rulers of vampire society on the Chinese mainland, the Korean Peninsula, and much of Southeast Asia, but their home was considered a holy place of philosophy, reason, and diplomacy. They were eight ancient rulers who had given up conquest and imperial pursuits for statesmanship and peace.

The elders were served by Taoist daoshi, orders of monks and nuns who venerated the elders as the highest manifestation of balance in the universe. The palace and the monastery were in turn supported by a community of humans who farmed and fished around the island.

Violence was nearly unheard of, and crime was nonexistent.

Tai guided them into a tearoom that overlooked a lush interior garden of mossy stones, ferns, and orchids. A teapot and three cups were already in place on a low table surrounded by comfortable cushions.

"There has been a theft on the island, and not a minor one," Tai said.

"What kind of theft?" Ben asked.

"A very valuable seal was stolen from one of the gates to the palace." Tai sat. "Perfectly excised from its wooden frame."

"The jade dragon was taken?" Tenzin asked. "How?"

"No, not that one." Tai looked at Ben. "Penglai has two docks with two gates—the Jade Dock, which leads to the main gate at the front of the elders' palace. That's the one most visitors use."

"That's the one I remember," Ben said. He'd only been to the island once as a human, but he pictured the bustling dock and the cobblestone road that twisted up the island leading to the front of the palace.

"There is also the Pearl Dock and Pearl Gate," Tai said.

"It's a smaller dock on the southeast side of the island, one that is used by our supply islands and some diplomatic visitors from the south and the east." He raised the teapot and poured into the three cups. "It's a dock and gate that have recently been undergoing renovations because we are expecting a large state visit from Sina, the ancient ruler of the South Pacific—"

"Really?" Tenzin sat up with interest. "I've never met her." She glanced at Ben. "Sina is famously reclusive and rarely leaves her islands."

"She is," Tai said. "But she's also extremely close to her daughter, Mahina, who is both her public face and mated to one of the elders here."

Ben frowned. "Wait, so Sina's daughter is mated to an elder here? Who?"

"Han Xiang," Tenzin said. "Water vampire. Very old. They only see each other for a month or two every year, but they've been mated for over seven hundred years now, so that's probably more than enough for both of them."

Tai shrugged. "I've always thought Mahina would prefer living here, but her obligations to her sire are numerous."

"Mahina usually comes here for a month this time of year," Tenzin said. "But Sina is coming with her this time?"

"Yes, for only the third time in history, which makes the theft of the Pearl Seal a huge problem."

Tenzin's eyes went wide. "They stole... What?"

"The Pearl Seal."

"You mean Mahina's Eye?"

"The whole seal, Tenzin."

Ben's own mate was an accomplished thief herself, which made her expression more than a little alarming.

"But *how*?"

Ben held up a hand. "What is the Pearl Seal?"

"A gold dragon approximately a foot across with a massive black pearl placed as the eye," Tai said. "The gold dragon was set into a carved jade border that was then set into the carved wooden gate over the eastern entrance to the palace. The dragon and the jade border were stolen."

Tenzin continued the explanation. "The pearl was a gift from Sina to Mahina and Elder Han on the occasion of their mating ceremony. Elder Han then had the pearl set into the gold dragon that adorned the gate facing the direction of Mahina's homeland to honor his mate."

"Elder Han is the only one of the elders who has taken a mate so publicly with so many political implications," Tai said. "I do believe they are genuinely fond of each other, but it is also a political union. Since their mating, Sina's territory and Eastern Asia have traded with very few complications. It's not a formal treaty, but..."

Tenzin turned to Ben. "It's an understanding. The fact that the Pearl Seal has been stolen is a huge loss of face for Penglai."

"And with Sina's visit happening sometime in the next two weeks, the elders don't have much time to find it."

There was a tap at the door, and a human servant poked her head in. "Master Tai?"

"Yes, Jing?"

"Elder Zhang has requested that Master Benjamin and Mistress Tenzin attend him in the elders' private garden after they have refreshed themselves." The young woman offered a hasty bow to both Ben and Tenzin. "I would not bother you, but the note came from the elder himself."

Ben felt his stomach drop and knew their planned holiday to celebrate the hundredth birthday of a beloved servant in their sire's household had just taken a very complicated turn.

Shit.

Tai smiled. "Thank you for relaying the message, Jing." He turned to Ben and Tenzin. "I can't offer a response for you."

Tenzin's face was wooden. "It wasn't a question to be answered, was it?"

Tai took a breath. "No. It wasn't."

Ben reached for her hand. "Let us get changed out of our travel clothes." He looked at his mate and caught the edge of simmering anger in her eyes. "Tell Zhang we'll be with him shortly."

Chapter Three

Unlike the formality of the great hall, the inner courtyard garden of the palace had many private corners, serene walkways, and secluded meeting spots. Tenzin had once danced along the taihu stones in the garden, following a brooding Benjamin when he'd been trying to avoid her. He'd been human then and angry with her for leaving him in Puerto Rico after a job finding pirate gold.

He'd brought a woman to Penglai his first visit there, a human who was in love with him, though Ben had never acknowledged it.

You left me. You're the one who ran away.

He'd hissed the words into her ear those many years ago, and the thought briefly floated into her mind that if she hadn't drawn him to Penglai those many years ago, he might still be human. His life might have been different.

But fate had different plans for both of them, and she wasn't a creature who ruminated; it wasn't her way. She hadn't foreseen the turn that Ben's fate had taken, but then there was much she hadn't seen. Or hadn't wanted to.

She halted when she saw the gathering of eight vampires on a wide bridge crossing a frozen pond.

It was winter in Penglai, and a dusting of snow had fallen the day before. Frost had kissed the garden, turning bare trees into crystalline statuary.

Statuary. Not unlike the eight vampires waiting for them. They sat on low stone seats that lined the bridge, all robed in formal white, the color of death for the elders who had conquered it.

Ben warmed his hand and put it in the small of her back. "They're waiting."

"Let them wait."

His thumb brushed against her in a gesture that was likely meant to be soothing. "Tiny—"

"We owe them nothing."

"We owe *him* our lives."

Or something of the sort. Tenzin had long stopped caring what her sire thought of her—she had paid for her own life in blood and fire—but when she'd come to Zhang with Ben's broken body, he had acceded to her demand. Zhang had sired Benjamin to air, and for that?

For that she would crawl on her knees across stone.

Ben stepped forward, the superior politician, and she followed him.

"Immortal elders." Her mate spoke as they drew near to the bridge. "We are honored that you have requested our company." He gave the precise bow that Tai had taught him when he was taking etiquette lessons.

"Welcome, Benjamin, my son." Zhang stood from the low stone seat. "And welcome, my daughter."

Tenzin inclined her head but said nothing.

Zhang continued. "Tenzin and Benjamin have arrived in Penglai only tonight as part of the celebrations for my oldest human servant, Erdun."

The Immortal Woman, Xe Xiangu, spoke. "Erdun is an honorable human. It is very generous that you celebrate him, Elder Zhang."

"He is marking a century in human years," Zhang said. "Quite long for a human."

All the elders murmured their approval at Zhang's generosity, and Tenzin managed to refrain from sneering.

Yes, how *generous* and *magnanimous* her sire was to give the hundred-year-old human who'd dedicated his life to serving her father a birthday party. As if it wasn't the least he could do to honor a man who had given his life to serve an immortal court.

As if reading her thoughts, Ben reached down and gripped her hand, squeezing lightly.

"Further, it is an honor for my household that both my children have come to celebrate the human Erdun," Zhang said. "Clearly fate has brought them here at this time."

A vampire to Zhang's right spoke, a slim, handsome man with classically Han features and two silver streaks in his hair at the temples. It was Lu Dongbin, the political leader of the group. "Mistress Tenzin and Master Benjamin, your arrival on Penglai has come at an auspicious time for the elders."

Tenzin finally spoke. "Because of the theft?"

Dead silence.

Heavens above, it was so satisfying to do that. Tenzin barely suppressed her smile. She let the awkward silence stretch. Sadly, Ben jumped in to smooth the wrinkle in her etiquette.

"We learned of this violation against the island only an hour ago, and it is... all we can think about," her mate said. "We were shocked that anyone would disturb the sanctity of Penglai." He paused for effect, touching his hand to his chin as if deep in thought. "If there were a way that Tenzin and I could help, I wish we could learn it."

Zhang looked amused but not disapproving. Tenzin was impressed; she hadn't thought Ben would frame the offer of help in that way, which would force the Eight Immortals into asking them for their assistance instead of Ben and Tenzin offering it.

The latter option was what she'd been expecting, and it wouldn't have been forgotten, but by making the elders formally request their help, they would earn a favor in the court of Penglai, not a small thing in any way.

Lu Dongbin's eyes met each of the seven other elders in turn before he turned back to Benjamin. "Your skill in the retrieval of valuable objects is well-known, Benjamin, son of Zhang. We know that you and Tenzin were instrumental in the retrieval of the Laylat al Hisab and other valuable treasures."

An elder in shadow spoke. "You have also retrieved an object of legend and unknown power," the vampire said. "The Bone Scroll."

Low murmurs of acknowledgment in the night air.

Ben's status as keeper of the scroll wasn't widely known,

but she wasn't surprised the elders had learned of it. They had spies everywhere, even in the mountain caverns of Ethiopia.

"Your most recent job in Mumbai was well conceived." The elder who spoke appeared to be the youngest, but they were actually one of the oldest. Lan Caihe, fire vampire and known mischief-maker on the council. "The cache of weapons was returned to the original owner, was it not?" Lan turned to his right and spoke to the Immortal Woman. "They had been stolen and placed in a large museum collection."

Murmurs of understanding from around the bridge. What ancient vampire hadn't had a cache of weapons, valuables, or documents taken by curious humans and stuck rudely into a museum exhibit?

"In a venture such as retrieving the Pearl Seal," Lu Dongbin said, "you appear to be uniquely equipped. The Elders of Penglai prefer to have someone from within the court retrieve the seal, and as you are children of Elder Zhang, we would ask your assistance."

As Tenzin had stated before, it wasn't really an ask. They couldn't say no, not without offending their sire and pissing off eight of the most powerful vampires in Asia.

"However," Elder Lu continued, "as this particular theft touches one of our company in particular ways, Elder Han Xiang has asked that you include his own chief of human guard in your company."

Tenzin felt an automatic objection jump to her lips, but she clamped them shut. Han wasn't an unreasonable vampire, and the pearl from the seal had been a gift from his mate's clan.

Further, the chief was a human. Humans could do things in daylight while vampires were limited.

She glanced up at Ben, who nodded.

"Elder Han's offer is generous and wise," Tenzin said. "We would be happy to meet this human and take him on as an associate in this venture."

"Excellent." Zhang clapped his hands. "Then it is settled. You, Ben, and Jae will find the Pearl Seal, return it to Penglai, and bring us the thief to punish."

Oh, Zhang.

Tenzin could already hear the objections to the last command bursting from Ben's softhearted conscience. She gripped his hand, squeezed it, and turned to Elder Han. "Please have your human join us in Zhang's quarters tonight. Will that be possible?"

"Of course," Han said with a polite bow. "And I expect that you will keep us informed of your progress."

"Certainly." Tenzin bowed again, turned, and dragged Ben with her.

"Did we just agree to be bounty hunters?" Ben hissed. "I agreed to retrieving a piece of art, not handing over a human or a vampire to their tender mercies."

"Just keep walking," Tenzin said. "We'll figure it out when we find the seal. Who knows? It could be a horrible vampire that you'll be happy to let them torture."

"I doubt it." His jaw was locked in a stubborn line. "Come on. Let's go meet this Jae."

WHAT HAD HE DONE?

What had he *done*?

The black swirl of the dragon's eye accused him, and the man shivered.

What have you done?

He'd taken the seal from the gate with no damage; it was perfectly intact and safe, wrapped in a woolen blanket he stored beneath the simple bed in his home. The small dwelling was perched on a cliffside overlooking the ocean, and the scent of the sea and the sound of the waves were his constant companions and his professional bane.

No wood was immune to the endless salt air of the sea, not even those hardwoods he was given to maintain the palace gates, walls, and various necessary tools and trimmings that were not made of stone.

He was no one and one of many, a bustling ant who performed the tasks that his father and his father had completed before him. He was one of the hundreds of workers who maintained the holy palace of the Eight Immortals.

He stared at the accusing eye of the dragon and shuddered, knowing he would face the wrath of the elders and the sharp hammer of fate.

But it would be worth it. It would all be worth it if he succeeded.

A small knock came from the outer room, and he turned to it. He rapped back on the wall twice, then carefully rewrapped the seal and slid it back under the bed, placing storage baskets in front to block the bundle from sight.

Not that anyone came to his home. He was no one.

No one to anyone but her.

He walked out of his bedroom and toward the small knock, closing the bedroom door behind him.

———

BEN AND TENZIN WALKED BACK TO ZHANG'S QUARTERS. Ben was walking through every step of the conversation and trying to figure out where he'd lost control.

Dammit, he wasn't handing anyone over to the elders; he didn't work that way. They found the art and then returned it. There was no retribution, no revenge. It was a simple exchange of property, and he wanted nothing to do with whatever form of "justice" the Elders of Penglai wrought.

He'd been a thief—some might say he still was—but he'd never stolen anything without a reason. Unless this thief was trying to cause a war or break a treaty, he knew whoever had taken the Pearl Seal probably had their reasons, and he wasn't going to judge.

They arrived back at Zhang's front room to see Tai sitting with a tall human with broad shoulders, a neat black cap of hair, and a military bearing.

The human stood as soon as he saw them, bowed to forty-five degrees exactly, and straightened. "Mistress Tenzin, Master Benjamin, I am honored to work with you. Elder Han has instructed me to provide whatever human help you require while also lending you my expertise in the current state of Penglai's security, the threats against Elder Han, and the likely political motivations for this violation of Penglai sovereignty."

Okay, so Jae clearly thought someone was trying to break a treaty or start a war.

Ben cleared his throat, a human habit he couldn't seem to break. "Are we sure the motivations aren't... less complex? This was a very valuable piece of art sitting outside the palace on an island with no electronic alarms, not much physical security, and a lot of open space." He looked at Tenzin. "It's possible someone saw an opportunity and took it."

Both Jae and Tenzin looked at Ben as if he'd grown two heads.

Jae said, "It seems unlikely that anyone would violate the sanctity of the island and risk the wrath of the elders for... financial gain."

Spoken like someone who'd never really been poor.

Ben shrugged. "Okay, you're probably right. I know that crime is not common on the islands."

"It's nonexistent," Tenzin said. "I have my issues with the bowing people and my sire, but this is the safest place in the world for humans and vampires. There is no random violence on Penglai. It is forbidden."

"I grew up on the outer islands," Jae said. "My father is a grain farmer for the palace, and even on the outer islands, things like this don't happen. I can't remember a time when they have even locked their doors at night."

Ben definitely wanted more information about Jae's background, but for now he just went with it. He was clearly in the minority thinking that the motivations for this could be anything as mundane as poverty.

"Jae, welcome to the team." He stepped forward and extended his hand to the man. "We're still catching up, and we've just arrived, so why don't we plan to meet tomorrow night?" He glanced at a window. "Dawn is just a couple of hours away, but if you could spend the day putting a short briefing together, I'd appreciate it."

Jae looked at Ben, then Tenzin. "Very well." He bowed to Tenzin. "Mistress Tenzin." He nodded at Ben. "Master Benjamin. I'll see you promptly at dusk."

The man left and Tenzin turned to Ben. "He's a bowing person. They gave us a bowing person to work with."

"He's a military guy." Ben took her by the shoulders and pointed her toward their room. "Just relax and he'll relax too."

"If he keeps calling me Mistress Tenzin—"

"Just give him a chance, Tiny. You never know. You might even end up liking him."

Chapter Four

B en slept deeply on Penglai. He didn't know if it was the lack of electronics, the deep quiet of geographic isolation, or some instinctive affinity to the place where he first woke as an immortal. Perhaps it was all three of those things or something he hadn't identified yet, but he woke at dusk with a settled feeling in his chest and Tenzin wrapped around his body.

"Did you sleep?" he whispered.

"No."

He brushed away the pang of disappointment. He knew logically that he couldn't gauge her happiness or contentment by whether or not she slept, but he couldn't seem to stop asking.

Since Tenzin had told him she'd started sleeping a little bit after taking his blood, he'd linked her feelings of safety— and his success as a mate—with her ability to sleep.

She's on guard here because of her sire, because of the poli-

tics, and because of her history. This has nothing to do with you.

If he kept saying it, eventually he might believe it.

Ben wrapped his arms around her, kept his eyes closed, and enjoyed the sound of the rain hitting the tile roof of Zhang's compound. He could smell humans in the distance, bustling around the kitchen and the service corridors in the house. He heard someone enter his and Tenzin's bathroom from the service hallway and knew the hot water was being filled for their evening baths.

"Did you meditate?" He ran a hand up and down Tenzin's back.

"Some. Nima left her khaden loom here, so I've been working on a sleeping rug every visit." For Tenzin, weaving was a form of meditation.

"Good. That sounds good." He wasn't going to ask how long she'd been working on it. Knowing Tenzin, it could be ten years. The end product wasn't the point.

"Erdun came by and we visited. He's still very fit for one hundred. He shared a book of poetry he's been working on illustrating."

"He's still drawing?"

"I don't think he'll ever stop," she said. "Not until he dies. The poetry is my father's."

Ben's hand froze. "Oh?"

She snuggled closer, an unspoken request for him to keep petting her. "It was surprisingly insightful."

He ran gentle fingers through her hair. "Well, Zhang is six thousand years old. If he hasn't picked up some wisdom in that time, he's kind of a lost cause."

"That's one way of seeing it, yes."

He enjoyed the silence and the rain as soft footsteps passed in the halls. He was in the cocoon of Penglai Island, lying on a bed covered in silk sheets, voluminous pillows, and embroidered quilts. The platform bed was surrounded by thick curtains while his mate lay draped across his chest and a brazier chased the winter chill from the air.

He was about to drift into a waking dream when Tenzin lifted her head.

"Are you still thinking about last night?"

Ben narrowed his eyes. "I wasn't until you mentioned it. Thanks."

"You're welcome." She sat up and crossed her legs, his sarcasm completely lost. "You did nothing wrong, and I am impressed that you made them ask us. They will owe us a significant favor now, and one that only the elders know about. It was well done."

"Until the end."

"Ah." She raised a finger. "But that is Zhang. That is why I wasn't happy to enter into any agreement with our sire even though I knew it was likely inevitable. Zhang will always manage to push every boundary you have created. He'll do it in such a way that his will becomes inevitable and you are forced to agree. Last night was not a surprise."

He propped an extra pillow under his neck. "Is this the part where you remind me that he's a six-thousand-year-old general and I'm still wet behind the ears?"

Tenzin frowned. "Your ears are wet?"

He shook his head. "It's this thing that Caspar likes to say; I have no idea—"

"Is there a leak in the roof?" She leaned forward and put her hand on the pillow. "I don't feel anything damp."

"It just means I don't know what I'm doing. My ears aren't actually wet. It's a figure of speech, Tenzin."

"Oh." She sat up straight. "You know what you're doing most of the time. You're not a completely bald goat."

Ben blinked. "Bald... Did you just call me a bald goat?"

"I thought we were exchanging amusing sayings. And by bald goat, the saying is actually referring to a boy's testicles before they become hairy." She shrugged. "It makes sense in context."

"I'm not really sure how this conversation got here," he muttered.

"Just know that whether it had been you or I negotiating, Zhang would have managed to slip in some clause or task he knew we wouldn't agree with."

"If you were negotiating, we wouldn't be helping the elders at all."

She leaned forward and patted his cheek. "Exactly."

———

Jae had taken over a corner of Zhang's library while Ben and Tenzin washed and prepared themselves for the night. He had a large picture hanging up, a schematic drawing of the Pearl Gate with neat characters lining each side. Folders and binders were spread out on the table along with two large maps.

"Master Benjamin." He bowed to Ben again, exactly forty-five degrees. "And Mist—"

"No." Tenzin raised her hand. "I acknowledge and return your respect, Commander Min Jae, but I am not your mistress and you do not need to acknowledge me as such. With respect, I believe both Ben and I would prefer you use our given names only while we are working together to signify our unity of purpose and equality of mind and rank. Let you be Jae and us be Ben and Tenzin."

Jae looked slightly uncomfortable at the idea, but he looked at Ben, who nodded.

"Agreed," Ben said. "Really, just call me Ben."

"With respect, Elder Zhang will not approve." Jae glanced at Tai, who was setting up a tray of tea on another low table by the fireplace.

Tai looked up. "Commander Jae, please know that Elder Zhang understands and accepts his children's eccentricities and informalities as products of the outside world wherein they work. He will not be offended if you use Ben and Tenzin's given names."

Jae still looked uncomfortable. "If you insist, Mis... Tenzin." He bowed stiffly. "And Ben."

"And no bowing." Tenzin walked over to Jae and looked up. She barely reached the tall warrior's chest, but she radiated power. "I was born to nothing. Fate has led me on a tangled path, Min Jae, but do not bow to me, because anything that I have become has been at the whim of fate, and I do not take credit for my ancestors' luck." She patted his chest. "Understood?"

Jae nodded, but he did not bow again. "Understood."

She turned to the table. "This looks like a very comprehensive briefing."

Ben swallowed the words in his throat and ignored the aching part of his heart that wanted to lift Tenzin in his arms, kiss her senseless, and tell her she was extraordinary.

She was, but she wouldn't appreciate it in that moment.

He approached the table and looked at the drawings. "This is a picture of the seal?"

Jae nodded. "We don't have any photographs of it, so I think the building schematic is the best representation. It was drawn by the building administrators around a century ago." He began pointing to the picture. "The frame around the seal is made of carved mahogany, so it must be resealed and protected regularly from the salt air by carpenters on the island. The larger gate was also recently rebuilt in preparation for the state visit from Sina."

"So there has been more activity around the Pearl Gate than there usually is because of the rebuilding," Ben said. "Anyone out of the ordinary? Any contractors or craftspeople from off-island come in to reinforce the old structure? Any outside help?"

"With all respect to builders on the mainland," Jae said, "when it comes to traditional building techniques, there are no better experts than the builders and woodworkers here on Penglai. They have practices that have been passed down generations. No outside worker would be more knowledgeable in traditional woodworking."

"I'll take your word for it." Ben nodded and looked back at the schematics. The seal was at the top of the gate, at least eight feet in the air, at the bottom of the frame. "The thief would need a ladder."

"Of course."

"How much damage was there to the wood? Did they break it apart?"

"No," Jae said. "It looked like the thief did everything possible to avoid damage to the gate or the rest of the structure."

"May we go look at the site?" Tenzin asked. "I'd like to see it in person."

"Of course. For the moment, a canvas is covering the gate and the woodcarvers are already working to put a replacement seal into the space until the original is found."

Ben frowned. "What kind of replacement?"

"For now, simple mahogany. Nothing valuable. It will be a placeholder only." Jae motioned to the door. "Walk with me; it's not far."

They left Zhang's quarters and walked all the way around the elders' garden, skirting the center pond, the standing stones, and passing through the stone garden in front of Elder Cao's compound. The jagged rocks rose up, miniature landscapes of the mountainous region that was the earth elder's homeland.

Jae, Tenzin, and Ben cut through the near-silent corner where Lan Caihe made their home, not a servant or monk in sight, and walked along the service corridor that led from the elders' compound to the administrative offices on either side of the great hall.

"Forgive me for taking you through the service corridors," Jae said. "But I am assuming that you would prefer to remain discreet."

"You guess correctly," Tenzin said. "The softer our footsteps, the more we will learn."

Ben followed at the rear, learning new pathways to familiar buildings. The service corridors of the palace were a honeycomb of passageways and narrow hallways that were designed to be efficient, fast, and invisible.

If I were planning a job...

For the hundredth time, Ben considered the blind spot that both Tenzin and Jae seemed to have around the idea of this being the work of someone on the island. The artisans, servants, and monks who worked in the palace had trained their entire lives to be invisible unless they were needed. It was automatic for them to be overlooked.

He couldn't think of a better cover for a thief.

"This way." Jae led them down a straight, windowless hallway, but Ben could feel where they were. They were walking along the edge of the palace structure, and he could sense empty space below his feet and on the other side of the wall. The hallway ended in a small wood-paneled door that Jae opened.

They stepped into the exterior garden that framed the entrance to the great hall, and when Ben looked back, he saw the door they'd stepped through disappear into the side of the palace structure, hidden by careful design.

"The Pearl Gate is this way." Jae walked across the flagstones that led through the bed of clipped maples and sculpted cedar bushes.

They joined a path that directed them to the front of the great hall, but instead of turning right, Jae led them left, under a stacked gate that reminded Ben of coral reefs. The rough stone had been piled artfully and adorned with sun-bleached shells from conchs and giant clams, pebbles, and other seashells.

With the moss growing artfully and the garden beds around it planted with twisting, leafed plants and trees, the interior of the Pearl Gate appeared as nothing less than an underwater palace entry.

Jae nodded to the palace guards on either side of the gate, and one man stepped forward and opened one of the large wooden doors intricately carved with carp and eels.

They stepped through the gate, leaving the safety of the palace, and onto a great stone veranda. From the edge of the outcropping, Ben could see the dark sweep of the Pacific before him along with the tiny lights of a dock on the edge of the island that jutted just to his right.

If he craned his neck to the south, he could see the edge of golden lights that lit Penglai town crowded around the main road that led from the Jade Dock up to the Jade Gate.

Tenzin walked to his side. "It's a stunning view."

"Is it just forest?" He floated up from the carved stone on the veranda into the air and out over the island, turning his back to the sea and following a pathway that was just wide enough for a carriage. "This pathway leads down to the Pearl Dock?"

Tenzin followed him into the air. "Only a few would use the Pearl Gate. Formal parties coming from the southeast, but that's about it."

"And the dock?" Ben turned to the dock and saw glittering lights in the distance. "Those are the islands Jae was talking about?"

"Yes. Penglai has five islands in the chain. The others are

smaller, less developed, and mostly used to house people, grow grain and vegetables for the palace. Raise animals. Fish. The outer islands use the Pearl Dock to supply the island." Tenzin pointed at a narrow road that led along the coast. "But they unload on the dock and then take the road into Penglai town. They don't go up to the palace this way."

Ben flew back to the landing that overlooked the sea and up to the gate to inspect the space where the seal had been. The area around the seal was delicately carved, and if he hadn't known there was supposed to be a great round seal there, he might have missed the damage entirely.

"Whoever did this was careful," he said. "They didn't want to damage the gate or the seal."

Jae stood below them. "The consensus among Elder Han's staff is that whoever did this wanted to create a state incident to interfere with Han and his mate's announcement."

Tenzin and Ben shared a look.

Have you heard about an announcement?

Obviously not.

Tenzin shouted down. "What announcement?"

Jae looked at the humans and vampires milling around the gate and trying to patch the damage. "Perhaps we can move to a more... private location to discuss this part."

Chapter Five

Thursday night was a market night in Penglai town, so Jae, Ben, and Tenzin strolled from the Pearl Dock through the eastern fishing village and into Penglai town where Ben soaked everything in like a tourist, from the bundled children running through the village—their warm breath puffing out like smoke in the frigid night air—to the women crouched by sizzling vats of oil where they fried potatoes and wooden sticks of crispy fish skin and meatballs.

The chatter of gossip and the dancing dialect of Mandarin that was known only on Penglai surrounded Tenzin. She felt a surge of affection for this place. Not the palace overseen by gods but this small pocket of traditional life clinging to shores that were battered by modernity.

There were mobile phone towers now, rising like metal claws on the mainland, and their signal just reached to the edge of the islands. The protection of isolation and immortal guardians felt tenuous and temporary in a way that it never had before.

"Do they do this every night?" Ben asked her.

"Thursday and Sunday," Tenzin said. "Monday is a resting day. Tuesday and Saturday are for the day markets." She smiled at him. "No vampires allowed."

"Do the people here...?" He frowned. "I mean, do they own their houses? The shops? How does that work?"

"What does it mean to own anything?" Tenzin asked. "They built it, and as long as it serves the community, it is theirs." She looked over her shoulder. "There's not really such a thing as ownership here. They don't need it."

"Is there a school?"

She nodded. "The monks and the nuns run it. All the children on the island can go."

"But they don't have to?"

Tenzin smiled at his modern sensibilities. "Are you going to tell the fifteen-year-old boy who wants to be a fisherman that he needs to spend years studying mathematics and philosophy before he can become a fisherman? Or are you going to let him study as long as he and his family want, then allow him to follow his own path?"

A group of children ran through, nearly knocking Tenzin over, and she heard a squawk from a group of older women chatting on a stoop.

"What are you doing?"

"Apologize to the teachers."

"Are you bears or are you children?"

"What happened to your manners?"

The three children ran back to Tenzin and Ben, their cheeks red and their eyes shining. All three of them bowed and spoke over each other.

"We are sorry, Lǎoshī."

"Forgive us."

"Please forgive our ignorance, Lǎoshī."

The panting children looked up at her with dancing eyes, and Tenzin could barely keep herself from laughing.

"Thank you." She squatted down and touched their foreheads. "And thank you for listening to your aunties. Be careful not to fall when you play."

"We will, Lǎoshī!"

"Thank you, Lǎoshī!"

"Teacher?" Ben asked.

"It's the traditional way that children address vampires on the island unless it's an elder, but most of the elders don't come to the village." She saw the eyes following them through town. "Most vampires don't come here either. Elder Li is probably the one who visits most because he's an herbalist and he consults with the human doctor here."

Jae added, "Elder Lu Dongbin's son Myung is the chief boatman and magistrate in Penglai town. Other than Myung, it's rare for the children to see an immortal." Jae gestured to a brightly lit building with red lanterns and a large green flag hanging from the corner of the roof. "Let's get a drink in a private room."

The tavern in Penglai town was the oldest on the island. Though Tenzin knew her father and his compatriots valued temperance, meditation, and sensual denial, they also knew that their island was staffed not only by Taoist monks but fishermen, builders, blacksmiths, tanners, weavers, and every other kind of tradesperson needed to run an island to imperial standards.

And those tradesmen and women needed a beer.

Jae waved at the tavernkeeper behind the bar, and the man pointed toward the back corner. Humans glanced at them with interest as they passed, then quickly looked away. Palace business was no business of theirs.

They found a private room that was little more than a table with benches around it, a warming brazier on the wall, and a door that shut. Jae ordered three beers and a bottle of the local baijiu, a snappy, sesame-scented rice alcohol that Elder Li had perfected centuries before.

Jae sat with his back to the wall and his eye on the door, keeping his voice low as he explained what he'd meant by Elder Han and his mate's "announcement."

"Elder Han and Mistress Mahina have been patient for centuries, Mahina bowing to her sire's demand that she remain the public face of the Pacific court and allowing Sina her isolation and time with her many children. She has a large clan; Mahina is the oldest and most politically experienced. It was Sina's mate's idea that Mahina take over the running of the court and the regular administration, only bothering them for the most serious cases."

Tenzin nodded. "All this is known."

"What is not well-known is that Sina's mate Ayal, who is from the east, has not made life pleasant for Mahina." He bit his lower lip. "It is not my way to speak ill of any elder, but my master has made his displeasure known, and Mahina has been quietly putting the court in order to be administered by her eldest child, a son named Kamaka. Kamaka is loved by Sina and will be a better balance to Ayal."

Ben caught on immediately. "Leaving Mahina to join Elder Han in Penglai."

"Finally." Jae nodded. "This is a very delicate negotiation that has been decades in the making. The last thing Elder Han wants is for Sina to see Mahina as leaving her mother's court for her mate's and shifting loyalties."

"Ayal is from Taiwan," Tenzin said. "Is that correct?"

Jae nodded. "Some have speculated that he would like Sina to more closely align with growing powers in the south rather than the northern elders. If you consider the theft of Mahina's Eye and the Pearl Seal along with Mahina's careful plans to leave her mother's court and move to her mate's, you can see how the combination of these... incidents could cause a break in the long-standing relationship between Penglai and the South Pacific region."

Causing a shift of Sina's attention and affection to the south, where her mate was more aligned.

The south.

Tenzin sighed.

Ben narrowed his eyes. "Wait a minute. The Elders of Penglai rule the majority of Asia, so who in the south would...?" He turned his eyes to Tenzin. "No."

Tenzin opened her mouth, then closed it.

Ugh. Why did he always have to show up at the most inconvenient times? Annoying pirate.

"Tenzin." Ben's voice was a low growl. "Tell me it's not him."

Well, this was going to get complicated.

"Cheng." Tenzin sighed. "Sina's mate would like her to shift her allegiance to Cheng."

Jae led them out of the tavern and toward a narrow road that led up the hill from Penglai town. "The torch at the top of the hill means Myung is at home, and he'll know much more. After all, there is more than one possibility presented in the brief I put together tonight. I mean, Jimmu and Matsu have long had a tenuous relationship with Pacifica. As they exist right now, they are taking in minimal tariffs from South Pacific trade, and I know Matsu would like to change that."

"The rulers of Okinawa and greater Japan are side players in this," Tenzin said. "Though I agree we should see what Myung says."

"We're forgetting wind vampires," Ben muttered. "All Myung can tell us is who came by boat, and you and I know better than anyone sneaking onto an island by air is more than possible even when that island is guarded by wind vampires."

He was sulking. Of course he was sulking. Ben and Cheng had never been friends, and even though Ben was her mate, he was keenly aware that Cheng had been her occasional lover for centuries.

"We should keep an open mind," Jae said. "No one wants to disrupt southern trade for spurious reasoning."

"No one wants to disrupt southern trade at all," Tenzin said. "That's why he's still there, plotting away, counting on favors he hasn't earned and skimming tax money from Penglai elders."

Ben said nothing. He didn't seem to care that Cheng

didn't know his place in the immortal political realm; he simply disliked the man.

Why? Because he'd given Tenzin more orgasms over the years? As if that meant anything in the greater scheme of things.

They walked up the cobblestone path, following the torches that led to a house that was far more like the traditional island houses than the palace at the top of the hill.

Myung's home was made of heavy stone mortared in place so the thick walls held up an angled roof of tightly bound thatch that swelled in the salt air and kept the interior dry and cozy. It sat in a curve of the cliffs overlooking the fishing village below and Penglai town to the left.

It was a horseshoe-shaped structure that combined the unique architecture of the island people with the grandeur of the palace above. In the center of the front courtyard was a tile-roofed glass house filled with tropical greenery even as the courtyard around it was dusted with snow and frost.

Tenzin had never been to Myung's home before, barely acknowledged him unless she had occasion to ride the stately red-sailed boat he used to formally ferry dignitaries visiting Penglai from the mainland.

"Master Myung!" Jae called from the curved cobblestone walkway in front of Myung's home.

Tenzin waited with Ben silent at her back. She knew he was angry that Cheng might be involved, but Tenzin doubted that her old friend was entangled in this theft. It was too twisted and underhanded. When Cheng wanted something, he confronted it directly. He could be deceitful for sure. He lied and twisted stories to suit his purposes.

But infiltrating the sacred island of the elders, stealing an important cultural and political treasure to drive a wedge between an old enemy and a wanted ally?

Actually, it would be fairly ingenious. Cheng might not dream it up, but his right hand, Jonathan? That was a distinct possibility.

The front door of Myung's house opened, and a young woman's head popped out. She spotted Jae, Tenzin, and Ben; then she held up a hand and ducked back inside.

Seconds later, a dark-haired man with pale, immortal skin and a classically handsome face stood at the door, wrapped in a quilted Korean-style jacket. Myung waved them into the house.

"Tenzin!" He spotted her and bowed deeply. "I heard you were visiting the island."

"Will you stop?" Tenzin smiled and stepped forward. "It's good to see you, Myung."

"What are you doing out in this cold?" He waved them inside. "Come in. My housekeeper will make us some tea."

"Thank you." Tenzin led the way into Myung's house, slipping off her muddy shoes and sinking her feet into the warm house shoes that Myung's servant provided.

Jae and Ben followed her from the entryway as she stepped up onto a heated floor where a human servant was laying out tea in the middle of comfortable curved couches that ringed a low table. Through the back door, she could see another servant adding wood to the stove that heated the kitchen and the floor of Myung's house. She sat across from him and waited for Ben and Jae.

"Would you care for more than tea?" Myung waved two

servants over, both young women dressed in Korean styles who bowed and turned their necks to the side, indicating they were available for feeding.

Ben sat next to Tenzin. "We fed at dusk, but thank you."

Tenzin had been tempted, but Ben was right. She wasn't hungry, just feeling a little irritated with her mate's mood. That was hardly a reason to bite someone unless it was Ben.

Jae stood next to them, unsure where to sit. Myung motioned to his right where a shorter cushion had been placed next to the table.

It sat lower than the couches, and Tenzin was keenly aware that Myung was reinforcing status with Elder Han's man. He might have been Elder Han's human commander of security, but Myung was the son of Elder Lu, chief magistrate of Penglai town and boatman of the Eight Immortals. Myung and Jae were nowhere near equals.

"Thank you, Master Myung." Jae's face revealed nothing. "As Elder Lu likely informed you, Master Ben and Mistress Tenzin will be assisting the elders in finding the Pearl Seal, and I have been assigned as their human associate."

"Of course." Myung directed his attention toward Tenzin. "I'm not surprised they asked for your assistance. Your reputation—and your mate's—is well-known. It was a wise decision."

Ben leaned forward as Myung's servant set out a delicate arrangement of fresh fruit next to the tea. "I don't think we've formally met." He reached out a hand. "Benjamin Vecchio."

"We did meet, but it was when you first came to the island, and I believe you had a little more than a boatman on your mind." Myung's smile was genuine as he shook Ben's hand. "It's good to see you again."

Myung served tea and handed a cup to all his guests, including Jae, before he sat back and sipped from his own fragrant, steaming cup. "I believe I can guess why you are here."

"We need to know who exactly was on the island when the Pearl Seal was taken," Tenzin said. "I know the harbormaster keeps records that would go to you."

"Of course. I have already looked them over myself," Myung said. "There was a period of two nights and a day when the Pearl Seal could have been taken. Carpenters have been working on the gate in preparation for Sina's state visit, so we know the seal was intact when the men finished with it Sunday evening. No outer guard was at the Pearl Gate the first night, so we have no way of knowing if it was taken then or the following night, Monday."

"So there's a thirty-six-hour window for the theft?" Ben asked.

Myung nodded. "More or less. The damage to the gate was reported to the dockmaster of the Pearl Dock at dawn of the second day, which was Tuesday."

"And who reported it?" Ben asked.

"A fisherman's son."

"Interesting." Ben frowned. "What made him walk to the Pearl Gate? He and his father would have been unloading at the dock, correct? That's quite a ways from the gate."

Myung smiled. "If you can believe it, the young man had a dog that jumped off the boat and went chasing rabbits when they docked. A puppy he's been training to work on the water with him. The boy followed the dog up the hill and saw a ladder leaning against the gate. He was curious, went closer to look, and reported the damage to his father. His father called the dockmaster, and the master sent a message to me."

It was as reasonable an explanation as any. Tenzin didn't doubt Myung's story. They were lucky they only had thirty-six hours to account for. Since the Pearl Gate was rarely used, the theft could have happened in a much larger window of time. Perhaps the thief had been counting on that.

"So who was on the island?" Tenzin asked. "In that thirty-six hours."

"Other than the usual comings and goings from the outer islands?" Myung set down his mug. "Three entries of note. There was a grain ship that landed from the mainland—our harvest this year was less than anticipated and we had to import some wheat. Those shipments were done by our own vessels from the outer islands though, so no outsiders were on the island. There was also a contingent of scholars from Jimmu's court who were consulting with my sire about an ocean plastic-cleanup project."

"Scholars only?" Ben asked.

"The usual number of security with them, nothing that seemed excessive or out of the ordinary." His eyes moved to Tenzin. "And one other boat. A trading partner from the south negotiating tariffs for the Tanggu port. Her boss has been paying through the nose to a corrupt official, and she was hoping to get some assistance from the elders."

Tenzin was silently cursing even as Ben asked the question.

"And who was the trading partner's boss?"

"I think your mate knows already." Myung couldn't stop his smile. "Old pirates up to their tricks again, Tenzin?"

"Cheng." Tenzin's tea burned her tongue. "Thanks, Myung. I better get that trading partner's name before we go."

Chapter Six

The first time Ben had been in the hold of a ship, he'd been tricked into accompanying a cache of gold and treasure Tenzin had taken from Kashgar, and he'd spent weeks on a Chinese freighter crossing the Pacific. The last time he'd been on a ship, he'd been nearly killed by an assassin from the Mediterranean, and Tenzin had taken him to Shanghai so Zhang could make him a vampire.

He stared at the wall of the luxury yacht that was taking them to meet Cheng in Shanghai. "You know, I really don't like boats."

Tenzin stretched out on the bed next to him, reading a magazine she'd snagged from the upper deck. "Good thing you're not a water vampire." She showed him a picture. "Who is this?"

"I think she's an actress." He frowned. "What is that magazine?"

"The only one I could find. There were no books on the

bookshelves. They were all decorative and they'd been glued together."

"Who does that?" He glanced at the magazine, which looked like some kind of glossy gossip rag from Europe. "She was in that big action movie last year with the aliens."

"Her teeth are strange."

"She probably got them capped or something." Ben had little interest in most movies since he turned immortal. He enjoyed watching football, going to live shows, and he could be a little obsessive about music. But most actors and actresses were strangers to him.

"What is capped?" Tenzin frowned.

"They file down your natural teeth and then put false shells over the top that are more perfect than your original teeth."

Tenzin looked horrified. "Were the teeth damaged?"

"Not usually. Just not uniform."

"Teeth aren't meant to be uniform." She shook her head. "What is wrong with humans?"

"So many things." He turned on his side. "Are you worried about this?"

"Capped teeth?" She had returned to staring at the magazine.

"No. Cheng."

She was still staring at the magazine. "Why would I be worried about Cheng?"

"Is it possible he stole the seal?"

"Oh yes." She set the magazine to the side. "It's very possible. Cheng wouldn't think of it, but it's the exact kind of thing that Jonathan would do."

"So why aren't you worried?"

"Because I don't think he did it." She reached for the magazine again, but Ben plucked it from her fingers.

"Explain."

She scowled at him. "It's *like* something he would do, but he wouldn't do this."

Ben tried not to roll his eyes. "Explain *more*."

She shifted to face him. "Staging a theft or some kind of similar sabotage to cause a rival to lose face with a business associate he wanted to poach is exactly the kind of thing Cheng would do. In fact, I can think of three occasions right now where he did something similar."

"But you don't think he did this?"

She sat up a little bit. "Despite what Cheng would have the world believe, he actually has an extreme amount of respect for the Eight Immortals. Maybe more than most vampires who pay them proper homage. He reveres their tradition, their history, and their philosophy."

It didn't match up with the image of Cheng Ben had in his mind. "So why is he always challenging their authority?"

"In business." Tenzin held up a hand. "In business, he does. And politics. He tugs at their reins in the business world because he doesn't think they should have influence in commerce the way that they do, but when it comes to who they are and what they stand for? Spiritually? Culturally? He would never admit it, but he reveres them."

Ben mused, "He did agree to help Zhang recover Arosh's treasure with pretty much zero argument."

"Because it represented a historic peace treaty between Western Asia and Eastern Asia." She reached for the magazine. "He might try to undermine Penglai when it comes to business, but he would never ever sneak onto the holy island and steal a relic that represented a historic alliance between an elder and an ancient. He would consider it sacrilegious."

That actually made sense. "So why did you agree with Jae that we needed to visit Cheng?"

She managed to snag the gossip magazine again. "My personal knowledge of Cheng is not evidence. Jae is our associate in this investigation and Elder Han's representative; he needs to reach his own decisions, and a visit to Cheng on this irritating boat will settle the matter."

Ben could feel his eyes begin to droop as the sun made an appearance on the horizon. "How much longer?"

"It's about sixteen hours from Penglai to Shanghai." She stroked a hand across his jaw. "Sleep, Benjamin. We'll almost be there when you wake up."

"I don't like boats, Tenzin."

"I know you don't." She set the magazine to the side and wrapped her arms around his shoulders as the day pulled him into oblivion. "I'll stay with you all day, and I won't sleep."

He fell into dreams of birch forests and lush green caves dripping with ferns. He stood on an open plain, cracked earth stretching between him and a distant figure. He floated up and up, the pale figure growing closer as the cold mountain wind pushed him forward.

The cracked earth spread, and glowing magma smoked the landscape, blurring his vision and scouring his eyes.

He felt her teeth at his neck, and her arms wrapped around his chest from behind. She whispered words he didn't understand, and he gripped her hands and pressed them to his heart, which burned like fire as it beat frantically beneath his ribs.

The blood of Temur...

———

HE WOKE AND SHE WAS NAKED AT HIS SIDE, HER FINGERS playing in his hair and her cheek pressed against his bare chest.

"I wanted your skin," she said simply.

Ben wrapped his arms around her and pressed her bare torso to his own. "You have it."

He'd given her permission to undress him when he was sleeping as long as they were completely alone. Sometimes her energy could only be calmed by this kind of direct contact. If she needed to ground herself in something, Ben wanted it to be him.

"What happened?" He held her close.

"Memories."

"Hmm." He kept one hand holding her tightly and allowed the other to stroke her hair back from her forehead. His dream ricocheted in his mind; he could feel her teeth in his neck. He urged her up his body and pressed her face to his neck. "I need your bite."

If he was going to have to face her ex-lover, he wanted her teeth marks all over him. She'd told him that she and Cheng never shared blood, so he wanted to throw her bite marks in his face.

Was it petty? Yes.

Did he care? No.

Besides, he always wanted her to bite him. If it were up to Ben, she'd sink her teeth into him every night, all over his body.

She rose over him, her fangs wickedly curving in her mouth. Her eyes were hooded with desire as he ran his fingers over her body, teasing her breasts and stroking her belly.

"Where?"

He turned his neck to the side, baring his throat to her.

She pressed her mouth to his neck and slid her teeth into his flesh.

His back arched as he gripped her waist. The heat rose on the surface of his skin, and the air around them ignited with amnis.

She drank from him, then licked at his neck like a satisfied cat, sealing the wound.

"Not too much," he whispered. He wanted them visible.

Tenzin's eyes met his, and she understood. The corner of her mouth turned up. "More?"

He was already hard, and he could smell her body ready for him, but he nodded. "More."

She hovered over him and bared his right shoulder where his neck met his collarbone, sinking her fangs into the hard muscle there, licking the blood away and leaving the wounds raw. Then she moved down his body, scraping her fangs along his chest, his defined abdominals, and licking lazily at the band of muscle that arrowed along his waist.

She straddled him and bent over, her arms framing his narrow hips as she brushed her cheek along his aching erection. She ran a fang delicately along the turgid flesh, and Ben nearly came just from watching her. But instead of taking him in her mouth or sinking her fangs into his inner thigh, she moved up and struck along the hard vee of muscle at his waist.

Ben gave a hoarse cry as Tenzin sank her teeth into his left side and pulled, nearly ripping his flesh in her ferocity. Her mouth bloody, she moved to the other side, leaving twin wounds visible at his waist. Then she licked them clean, moved up his body, and slid onto his erection with a satisfied sigh.

"Don't come yet," she whispered. "Not yet."

He groaned, but he managed to hold back from the brink.

Ben couldn't take his eyes off her. Her mouth was red with his blood, and the aching pleasure pain of her bite bloomed over his torso and neck. Her eyes were fire when she looked down, and he rose, sitting and gripping her hip with one hand as he pulled her down harder, moving her up and down his cock, working her body over his.

Her eyes were half-closed when she leaned her head to the side and bared her throat. She hooked one arm around Ben's neck and pressed him closer.

"Now." Her voice was a breathy moan. "Now, Benjamin."

His fangs ached in his mouth as he struck her neck and drank the rich blood that hit his tongue. He felt her muscles convulse around him, and he let himself follow her climax, chasing the heady pleasure of amnis, blood, and joined flesh.

She wrapped her arms around his neck, whispering something nonsensical into the air as Ben ran his hands up and down her back, easing her down from her peak.

He felt her blood in his body, her amnis running along his skin, through his nerves, and filling his mind with heightened awareness. The scents in the room were sharper. His vision even clearer. He felt every hair on his body rise to follow her fingers as they skimmed over his shoulders.

After an hour of more leisurely lovemaking, Ben heard a signal horn in the distance and a few seconds later, an answering sound.

He looked at Tenzin, her mouth, neck, and breasts covered in smears of blood.

That should not be as sexy as it is.

Ben shook his head and tapped her visible fang. "I'm thinking a shower might be a good idea."

The corner of her mouth turned up. "You're the one who wanted to show off."

"Thanks." He had half a dozen bite marks on his torso, and at least three would be visible even if he was wearing a long-sleeved shirt. "I think he'll get the message."

———

THE CAPTAIN PULLED THE YACHT UP TO A PRIVATE DOCK located in a luxury community south of the city and owned by Cheng. It was dotted with expensive villas and modern mansions overlooking the water and boasted a man-made beach, pleasure islands, and immaculate landscaping designed to appeal to the ultrarich of Shanghai. Hell, the ultrarich from any country on the globe.

Ben took note of various flags flying off neighboring boats as he floated from the deck of the Penglai yacht to the pristine white walkway where Jonathan, a British water vampire who acted as Cheng's second, waited for them.

"Benjamin Vecchio." Jonathan was so pale he nearly glowed in the moonlight, but his blue eyes appeared friendly. "It's been too long."

"It's been a while." He reached out before he remembered Jonathan didn't shake hands. "Is Cheng waiting for us?"

"He is." Jonathan's eyes lingered on Ben's neck, then caught a bite Tenzin had left on his inner biceps. "Is she joining us? He'll be expecting her."

"You know she does what she wants."

Jonathan's eyes pointedly looked at Ben's neck. "Obviously."

A gangplank was latched onto the walkway, and Jae walked across in the company of one of the ship's officers. They consulted quietly for a few minutes; then the officer nodded and returned to the ship, and Jae walked to Jonathan and Ben.

"Are you Jonathan?" Jae asked.

"I am."

Jae hit his forty-five-degree bow with his usual precision, and Ben saw one of Jonathan's eyebrows go up.

"I greet you in the name of Elder Han Xiang and extend my thanks for your cooperation in solving this mystery."

Jonathan turned his cool blue gaze back to Ben. "I'm still not clear on what this *mystery* is."

Ben didn't know quite how to broach the topic of Penglai suspecting Cheng of grand theft, so he folded his hands and said, "Why don't we wait for Tenzin so everyone is on the same page?"

"Very well."

A few silent minutes later, Tenzin joined them on the dock, her hair flying wild in the ocean breeze. She wore a long tunic and loose pants, both in black, and Ben's bite was immediately visible on the curve of her delicate neck, an angry red wound that she'd done nothing to heal.

As proud as Ben was to wear her marks on his body, he had a visceral and satisfied reaction to seeing her skin marred by his fangs.

Mine.

She wore his bite and a ruby ring on her left hand, the rich red stone winking in the moonlight like a gleaming drop of fresh blood.

"Jonathan," Tenzin said. "Thank you for meeting us on such short notice."

Cheng's man immediately turned and started walking up the dock as Tenzin fell into step beside him. "It *was* short notice; you got lucky. You know you're always welcome, but we've had meetings and trade negotiations every week for the past two months."

"That's a lot of time in the office for him."

Jonathan chuckled a little. "Not so much time for him. More for me. He sweeps in at the end, impresses or frightens them, then makes his dramatic exit."

"Still a pirate after all this time," Ben muttered.

"Exactly." Jonathan's eyes when he glanced over his shoulder were amused. "Just the legal kind these days. Mostly."

"The mostly is what we might need to discuss," Tenzin said. "There was an incident at Penglai when your last trade representative was there."

"Is that so?" Jonathan appeared to search his memory.

Jae almost jumped in with more information, but Ben put a hand on his arm and shook his head slightly. Tenzin was the best person to deal with Cheng.

"If it was recent, I suppose it could be Captain Sousa. Cristina Sousa," Jonathan said. "One of our captains from Macau. She had a meeting recently with one of Elder Lu's people about smoothing things out at the port. They were charging her excessive amounts to offload grain from Australia. A moderate amount of graft is expected for discretion, but it was getting out of hand. Cristina asked to meet with the elders personally, and if I recall correctly, her experience was positive." He glanced at Tenzin. "Was there a problem?"

"Not with Captain Sousa," Ben said. "Not that we were told. It was a routine visit."

They walked from the dock and onto a broad veranda where lamps highlighted lush tropical plants; proud traveler palms and blooming birds-of-paradise gave the veranda a private air even as it faced the open ocean.

"Come in." Jonathan pointed to an open pair of french doors. "Cheng is waiting."

Chapter Seven

Tenzin spotted the old pirate immediately. Splayed out on a low jade-colored sofa, he wore a pair of loose pants and a billowing shirt open halfway down his chest. Cheng rose when he saw her, his barrel chest, long hair, and beard marking him as the modern-day pirate he'd always been.

"Cricket." He opened his arms and walked forward to embrace her. "It's been too long."

She felt a jolt of amusement and familiar affection when she returned his embrace, then immediately after, a bitter thread of violence slipped through her mating bond with Benjamin.

He *hated* Cheng.

Tenzin stepped back and cocked her head. *Don't provoke him.*

Cheng raised an eyebrow. *Me?*

Ben's jealousy was unnecessary. Now that Tenzin had her physical need for touch met nightly by Benjamin, there was no need for her to maintain a physical relationship with Cheng. She had never trusted him the way she trusted Ben anyway, so it was far better that they were no longer lovers.

Cheng turned to Ben. "Vecchio, good to see you doing well."

"Cheng, same to you."

They shook hands in the Western fashion, and Tenzin could see both vampires sizing each other up.

Cheng took stock of the new vampire he'd known as a human. He could no doubt sense Ben's elemental power, which was raw and immensely dominant. Most vampires sired to air didn't learn how to fly for decades. Tenzin herself had been nearly one hundred before she took to the air.

Ben had woken his first night as an immortal floating over a bed.

Her mate was surveying Cheng, perhaps less impressed with the vampire now that he saw him with immortal eyes.

Cheng was wildly charismatic—it was what had made him such a popular pirate—but his elemental power was typical for a vampire his age. He was heavily muscled and carried himself with confidence, which threw many vampires off, but Ben was no inexperienced boy to be blinded by swagger.

The corner of her mate's mouth turned up, and she felt the kick of cocky energy drifting toward her.

Good. This was good. Perhaps he'd be less hostile if he and Cheng—

"What do you say to a duel?" Cheng grinned. "For old time's sake. I don't think we ever had the pleasure when you were human."

"That sounds great." Ben smiled.

Jonathan sighed. "Is this necessary?"

"Yes." Ben and Cheng spoke at the same time.

Cheng slapped his lieutenant on the shoulder. "Just a bit of fun, old chap."

Tenzin said nothing. Part of her wanted to put a stop to it, but the majority was too interested in how this confrontation would progress.

"So what will it be?" Ben asked. "Host's choice: jian or dao?"

Cheng spread his arms. "Are we on the water? Dao of course."

The curved broadsword was Cheng's weapon of choice and one that Ben had trained in, but not as much as Cheng had used it in actual combat.

"Dao it is." Ben nodded toward the veranda. "I'm assuming we shouldn't do this inside."

"I'll have the servants bring the weapons." He motioned Ben toward the french doors.

"Now, no flying." Cheng looked over and winked at Tenzin. "I've dueled your kind before."

Ben's smile was suitably enigmatic. "I very much doubt that."

Jae looked faintly panicked. "Mistr—I mean Tenzin—is this a good idea?"

"It's fine." She waved a hand. "Jonathan, maybe we can talk about Captain Sousa while they're stretching their arms."

"Of course. Shall we?" Jonathan ushered her out to the veranda as Ben and Cheng stripped off their shirts, servants quickly moved tables, and two men in black brought a large black case to the edge of the veranda along with a large stack of white towels.

For blood of course.

"So tell me again what this mystery is," Jonathan said. "I'll fill Cheng in when they're finished."

"Certainly."

Jae watched everything with wide eyes. "If I may, Mister Cheng may be giving a false sense of amiability with Ben. Is he—?"

"Sincere? Oh no," Tenzin said. "They'll both try to hurt each other quite severely."

Tenzin wished she could watch the fight with all her attention, but she needed to question Jonathan about the seal.

As Cheng and Ben took their weapons and examined them, they were also surreptitiously examining each other.

Her vicious, ripping fang marks were evident along the rise of Ben's waist, and Tenzin had to stop herself from staring. It was hard enough to keep her eyes from the marks on his neck and arms.

"It certainly appears that he's well-acquainted with combat," Jonathan said dryly. "And I am reminded why I'm so relieved we never became lovers."

"You're not my type," Tenzin said. "He is." She tore her eyes away from Ben. "What do you know about Han's mating with Sina's daughter?"

"Han Xiang and Mahina the water princess, legendary lovers." Jonathan smiled a little. "Not more than anyone knows, I suppose. Theirs was a political marriage that turned to a love match, and yet they spend most of their time separated by duty, not unlike a vampire Persephone and Hades if you will."

Jae looked at Tenzin, but she lifted her hand slightly and motioned for him to be quiet. "I will tell you in confidence and depend on your complete discretion when I say they are making some moves to change that situation. Mahina has served her sire's court for centuries but believes her son may be a good fit for the position going forward."

"Interesting." Jonathan seemed to consider the information, though no surprise showed on his face. "Perhaps not totally unexpected."

Ben and Cheng had chosen their weapons, taken their positions, and now began the duel. It started with swords laid flat across their arms as they bowed to each other. Then they backed up and the fight began.

The first strike of steel against steel answered any question Tenzin had about the lethality of the weapons. They were hewn to a very sharp edge.

Jonathan's voice brought her back to the conversation. "If it's the son I'm thinking of, her sire's mate won't like it, but it won't be a bad turn for our shipping agreement. We've cultivated relationships beyond the obvious, and both of Mahina's children are very competent leaders."

Meaning Cheng had allies with all the factions in Sina's court. A smart plan for a pirate and not an unexpected turn. Which made their motive even less than Jae had anticipated. Tenzin looked to the human to see if he understood, but his eyes were transfixed on Ben and Cheng's duel.

Jonathan turned to the dueling vampires. "Speaking of interesting."

Tenzin couldn't take her eyes off her mate. "Isn't it?"

"Do you think he realizes—?"

"Impossible to say." She leaned forward. "For him, it is as natural as breathing."

Though Ben wasn't flying, his feet only glanced across the ground. He moved with a fluid grace, almost like he was swimming in the air. His movements were faster; his sword moved with preternatural speed, as if the air itself were fighting his opponent.

He had a slash across one arm and it was dripping; his blood suffused the ocean air and made Tenzin's fangs grow longer in her mouth.

They circled each other, Cheng a master with his favorite weapon, and Ben a preternaturally gifted beginner.

The water in the air drew to the pirate's skin, and his long hair was tied back, whipping in the breeze that grew stronger with each passing minute. Ben might not realize it, but the wind had picked up and the waves were rising.

Jonathan stopped all pretense of discussion, his attention riveted on the fight.

Jae breathed out. "Incredible."

Both vampires bled from glancing wounds on their arms and chests. They spun with whip-fast speed around the clearing, faster than any human could move. Behind them, the ocean and the wind were locked in similar combat, the waves reaching up to grab at a whirlwind that had formed over the water.

Ben's arms were longer and his reach was impressive, but Cheng was fast, ducking under Ben's outstretched arm, sliding to the side and hitting the curved edge of his dao against Ben's thigh.

The wound seemed to have no effect on Benjamin at all. He turned, his shoulders rippling with lean muscle and his body twisting as he dodged a piercing thrust from Cheng's saber.

He lifted his arm and slashed down, pulling back at the last moment before he would have taken Cheng's left forearm.

Cheng's eyes darted to Ben's face, his eyes narrowing when he realized how close he'd come to losing a hand.

He backed away, spinning with a flourish and bringing his sword to meet Ben's blade in midair. "Draw!"

Both vampires froze, though the waves and the wind behind them had whipped up a squall. Water crashed along the dock as if a storm had descended on the harbor despite the crystal clear night sky.

A fine mist sprayed the entire veranda, the air whirling around Ben and lifting his hair, inching under his feet to cradle him.

"Magnificent," Jae whispered.

Truly, in that moment, with the air whipping the ocean into a churning mass, the mist spreading behind him, and his element holding him in its embrace, Ben appeared like the prince he was. His hair blew wild in the wind, his lips were parted, his element held him—it *was* him—and as he blew out a simple breath between his lips, the mist fled from the veranda, the air calmed, and he settled again on the ground.

Jonathan turned to her, his face an indifferent mask,

though she could see a slight tremble in the water vampire's hand. "I do hate when you're right about things, Tenzin."

Tenzin watched her mate as he bowed to Cheng and exchanged the usual pleasantries she'd taught him when he was younger. It was a friendly duel. Nothing had been won or lost.

Except that it had.

————

CHENG JOINED THEM WEARING A FRESH SHIRT AND DRY pants that hadn't been soaked by a violent ocean wind. He, Jonathan, Ben, Tenzin, and Jae sat in a more private study where a feast had been spread out, blood-wine had been opened, and a fire had been lit.

"Sina's mate has made aggressive overtures to those of us in the south, and I've been receptive," Cheng said. "But that doesn't mean I'm cutting ties with Mahina's people. Frankly, Ayal is a pain in the ass, impressed with his own cunning."

"And Mahina's son?"

"Kamaka has the tact of a shark, which means he has none." Cheng grinned. "I *like* him. He's forthright and he's not a schemer. He's predictable only because he serves his grandsire and their people. If he takes over from Mahina's careful leadership, that can only be a benefit to us."

Jonathan said dryly, "I'll take rude and honest over scheming and friendly any day. We entertain Ayal and his people, but if it comes to it, Sina's power will be behind those of her line, and her mate is not in her line."

"So you have no reason to try to sabotage the announcement of Mahina and Elder Han's reorganization?" Jae asked. "I ask only for clarity for my master."

"This theft you told us about?" Cheng's expression lost its amusement. "The island is a sacred place, as are any of the gifts and relics given to it. I may be a pirate, but I don't tempt the gods."

Ben asked, "Any ideas?"

Cheng frowned but said nothing, and Tenzin was happy to see that any animosity between the two seemed to have dissipated.

"I'd suspect Ayal's camp," Jonathan said, "but that would be a direct challenge to Mahina, and I don't think he'd take that route. He knows that if he pushes Sina, she will not side with him. He is her companion, not her blood."

Ben reached over, his fingers trailing down Tenzin's forearm until they danced around her ring, twisting it between his thumb and his middle finger. He stroked the soft flesh between her knuckles as he spoke.

"We may be looking too far afield."

Jae and Tenzin both turned to him.

"You know what I said from the beginning," Ben said. "This may be less complicated than we think. The motives might be much simpler and have nothing to do with politics."

Cheng nodded at him. "I agree with Vecchio. I'm a scheming thief by nature, but I truly can't see a political outcome from this that would benefit the perpetrator. No good can come from the theft of the Pearl Seal unless all one wanted was for the elders to lose face."

"And that," Tenzin said, "could be a very dangerous thing."

"Volatile," Cheng added. "I may tweak those who seek to bind me too tightly, but I would never presume that the combined power of the elders is something I could take on directly. I'm not a fool."

"If I may?" Jonathan turned his attention to Tenzin.

She nodded.

"I deeply respect the elders and their society," he said carefully. "The peace they have brought in the past few centuries has no equal in immortal history."

Ben said, "I'm sensing a but."

Jonathan gave a single nod. "In my experience, powers that are long established are not always the quickest to see unrest within their own walls."

Chapter Eight

Powers *that are long established are not always the quickest to see unrest within their own walls.*

Ben contemplated Jonathan's words en route to Penglai. Tenzin was perched on the front rail of the boat, and Ben was sprawled in a deck chair behind her, taking in the ocean air for as long as possible. While the night lasted, he could leave the wretched hold of the ship. Sitting on deck, Ben felt as if the wind were feeding him. It caressed his skin and curled through his hair, whispering secrets and energizing his amnis with every gust.

She turned and looked over her shoulder. "You're thinking about what Jonathan said."

How could she always read his mind? "Yes."

"He's an outsider."

"Aren't we?"

"Of course not." She turned and swung her legs toward him. "Penglai is in our blood. You woke there. Our sire founded it with his former enemies. We are as native to Penglai as any vampire in the world. Jonathan is not."

Ben frowned. "How did it come to be?"

"The islands?"

"Yes."

She looked into the distance. "I wasn't there for the beginning. I believe Zhang and Elder Li came first. The others followed. The islanders built the palace over time as a way to honor the immortals."

"Was the monastery already there?"

"I believe so. Or something like it. Penglai has always been a holy place."

Something about the whole setup was starting to bother Ben. He'd always just accepted Penglai Island as Zhang's kingdom before. He arrived by air, spent time in the palace, then flew away again. He didn't think about carpenters reinforcing ancient wooden gates, where the food came from that fed the palace compound, or how the wood arrived in the fireplaces every night.

But now?

Now he was looking, and maybe he was seeing what Jonathan had implied.

Was there unrest in Penglai?

Would the elders even see it if there was?

———

Two nights later, Ben and Tenzin met Jae again at the tavern in Penglai town. This time they were sharing a jug of the local beer, and Ben was enjoying the snappy herbal brew that had a hint of honey.

"I spoke to Myung again," Jae said. "He even allowed me to search the harbormaster's logbooks myself. I looked at the days after the theft of the Pearl Seal, wondering if there was anyone on the island who left for an unexpected trip to the mainland." He shook his head. "There was nothing."

Ben held up two fingers. "You're forgetting two elements."

Jae frowned. "What do you mean?"

"Water and wind." Tenzin leaned her elbows on the table. "A water vampire could simply swim to the island, steal the seal, and swim away again without alerting anyone. Same for a wind vampire. I come and go from the island at my leisure," Tenzin said. "No one tracks me."

"Of course the guards do," Jae said. "And there are guards in the water and in the air."

She smiled. "Do you really think I can't avoid them?"

Jae looked as if Tenzin had just told him Santa Claus and the Easter Bunny didn't exist. "So there is nothing secure about the islands?" His voice was barely over a whisper.

"I'm not saying that," Tenzin said. "Because the moment I interact with anyone, human or vampire, I come to the attention of the elders. And who is to say that Elder Li and Elder Cao cannot sense the moment my foot touches land?"

Jae relaxed a little.

Ben was betting that both the earth elders could sense any foreign amnis on their soil, but that still didn't take away from the fact that a wind vampire wouldn't have to set foot on any soil to steal the relic.

"I am scheduled to meet with Elder Han later tonight." Jae's eyes looked defeated. "My master will want to know our progress, but it seems that we have made none."

"I wouldn't say that," Ben said.

"Really?" Tenzin frowned. "I would."

"We know that Cheng didn't steal the seal," Ben said. "We have one less suspect."

Jae's eyes were wide. "That is... some progress. You are correct."

"Further, we got more insight into the dynamics in Sina's court. Jonathan and Cheng were being open with us. It sounds like Sina's mate and her daughter are fighting more than we realized," Ben said. "Is it possible that her mate, Ayal, is the one responsible for the theft? Could he be working with someone on the island?"

Jae nodded. "This is knowledge we didn't have before. I'll take this to Elder Han and see if he has any additional information. Being mated to Mahina, he may have answers to these questions that can help us in our investigation."

"Sounds good," Ben said. "Let us know what he has to say."

Jae finished his beer and left the tavern. Ben and Tenzin remained, a half-drunk jug of beer between them.

"You're quiet tonight."

Tenzin looked up from contemplating her beer. "You flexed your power openly when you were fighting Cheng the other night. Was that your intention or was it unknowingly done?"

Ben blinked. "Have you been thinking about this for two nights?"

"Yes."

"And you're just asking now?"

She frowned. "I wanted to consider my words."

Ben chewed on his bottom lip a little bit. "Does it matter if it was conscious or not?"

"Yes."

"Why?"

"One implies control, the other does not. You have power, but your control is still developing." She frowned. "We came at our elemental ability in very opposite fashion. When Zhang sired me, he was much younger, had many children, and I was not particularly powerful. I developed control over what power I had in order to use it most effectively."

It was the most she'd ever shared about her early life, and Ben wanted more. He doubted she'd be more forthcoming though. Tenzin tossed out details of her past like bread crumbs that were snatched away by the wind.

Ben said, "So unlike you, I got a whole lot of power very quickly when Zhang sired me because he's so old and hasn't sired any other children over the years."

"Yes."

Ben had wondered for years why that was. He had his suspicions, but he'd been reluctant to ask the questions. Something about the chaos of the tavern and the curtains around their booth made him bold. "Why?"

Tenzin's face showed no surprise; it was almost as if she'd been expecting the question. She probably had been. "Why did Zhang sire no other children in thousands of years?"

"Yes."

Her gaze never wavered, and Ben knew what she was

going to say before the words left her mouth. "He knew that I would kill them."

His heart felt as if it were made from lead. "Because you killed his other children."

"Yes."

"And their children?"

Her eyes were cold. "I killed those who needed to be killed, Benjamin. I will never regret it."

"And Temur?"

Now there was a flicker in the shadows behind her eyes. "Temur was one of Zhang's sons, yes."

"But it sounds like there may have been some of his blood who survived."

"It's a big world; it's possible."

Ben nodded slowly. "Do you know how the Sokholov fire vampire is connected to Temur?"

"Not yet." Tenzin's eyes grew warm again. "But I plan to find out. And when I do? I'll kill who needs to be killed. Do you disapprove?"

She'd told him she wanted to change, but how much change was truly possible when a soul was five thousand years old?

"Will it bother *you* if you do?" Ben asked softly. "Will it break your... New Year's resolutions?"

The corner of her mouth turned up. "You mistake growth for weakness. You have encountered Sokholov now. To allow the vampire to live and continue cultivating their chaos would be weakness."

"And what if Temur has other blood in the immortal world? What if he has descendants who don't even know who he was?"

Tenzin's face closed down. "Then I will consider if their lives are worthy."

"Should you be the judge of that?"

"I'm the only one with the right, and that right was born of the blood of my own children." She leaned forward and her eyes flashed. "I am not interested in *justice*."

"Then what are you interested in? Temur paid with his blood. You just told me that. Zasha Sokholov seems like a sociopath—I'm not worried about you taking them out. But some random vampire existing in the world with this Temur guy's blood? What would be the purpose?"

"Retribution."

"For something they had nothing to do with?"

"Zhang took my children; I took his. That is as close to *justice* as I am capable of, Benjamin. The debt that Temur owed me was paid in blood. It was a different time, and I will never apologize for who I was, then or now."

Could he live with that? Could he live with a mate whose moral compass was formed in a time when "an eye for an eye" was a progressive stance?

Could he live without her?

"I'm going to keep pushing you to grow," Ben said. "Because I love you and I've learned that forgiveness isn't weakness."

"If you try to change me, you will be disappointed."

"I can't change anyone; you can only change yourself." He reached across and took her hand. "But hopefully I can show you that change isn't always bad."

"And I'll show you that power is necessary. And mercy

isn't always the answer." She squeezed his hand. "Was the power you flexed with Cheng intentional?"

"Yes. I wanted to beat him and humiliate him because I was jealous." And it embarrassed him now—even acknowledging those feelings felt like weakness.

"Good." She smiled. "You need to do that more."

Ben frowned. "What? Tenzin, I'm not proud of the fact that I was puffing my chest out like a cocky kid. Jealousy isn't a good look."

"But strength is. You're seeing this the wrong way because you're young and still somewhat stupid."

He rolled his eyes. "I love you too."

"Thank you." She ignored his sarcasm. "You are moving through the immortal world with a reservoir of power bursting from you. Unless you want to be a paper tiger, you need to show that you can use it."

He let her words sink in because in his gut, he knew she was right. "Giovanni was an assassin before he was a scholar."

"You don't have the anger that he did. You'd make a terrible assassin." She raised a brow. "But yes. He was a feared killer before he was a scholar."

"So what are you trying to say?"

"You've been given an opportunity to demonstrate your power on one of the largest stages in the immortal world." She nodded. "When you see the opportunity to show what you can do, take it."

———

BEN WAS WALKING THROUGH THE GARDENS AN HOUR before dawn when he heard a scuffling in one of the flower beds. Immediately wary, he pulled a dagger from the hidden sheath in his pants.

Only to put it away when he saw the hunched figure of Elder Li Tieguai clomping out from the dense bushes.

Ben took a step back and waited for Li to walk to the path, a metal contraption held in the man's right hand. Though it had the appearance of a crutch, Ben knew the elder used it as a weapon, a digging instrument, and a prop to hide his power.

Of all the vampires on Penglai, Li Tieguai was the only one Ben would classify as ugly. He kept his figure hunched, wore robes that looked like old burlap sacks unless he was in the great hall, and never brushed or combed his patchy hair. His beard was scraggly, and his expression was permanently twisted so that it looked like he was constantly smelling something foul.

"Elder Li." Ben bowed deeply. "May I assist you with something?"

"No." The vampire growled. "The mint is particularly vigorous in that part of the garden, and one of my servants is having bowel problems. Do you want to help with his bowel problems?"

Ben blinked. "I'm not sure how I could help with that, Elder Li."

"Exactly, but I can." The vampire looked up at Ben. "You're Zhang's new son."

"I am."

"The one they want to find that gold dragon with the pearl eye."

"Yes, Elder Li."

"Have you found it yet?"

"No, sir."

The vampire harrumphed. "Well, that's not good for you, is it?"

"No, Elder Li."

"Just call me Li, for fuck's sake." The old man waved. "The rest of my *wise* brothers and sisters believe this is a theft to make us lose face. To make us look weak to Sina's people."

Ben's interest was piqued. "You don't think so?"

Li tossed a clump of dirty green leaves into a basket by the edge of the path. "I don't have a theory. It's a great gold dragon with a black pearl eye. Does it do anything useful?" He threw up a hand. "No! I don't give a shit about it."

"But you agree it will make the elders lose face if it remains lost?"

"Of course it will, but we have a little face to spare, don't we?" He wrinkled his nose. "What do you care about it, Zhang's son?"

Ben smiled. "Well, if nothing else, my sire gave me a task and I'd like to complete it."

Li shrugged as if it was as good an explanation as any. "So what's your theory?"

Ben took a chance on the irascible vampire's burst of honesty. "I don't think it was taken to make the elders lose face. I think it was taken because it's a giant chunk of gold and a massive pearl and they're worth a lot of money."

Li picked up his crutch and brought it down on the edge of Ben's shoe.

Ben didn't wince, but he wanted to. He stood completely still.

The elder pointed at him. "You're not stupid."

"Tell that to my mate."

Li waved a hand. "Your mate thinks everyone is more stupid than she is, and the irritating thing is, she's probably right." He started to wander off toward his section of the compound. "Look around you, Zhang's son. Have you looked at the islands? *Really* looked?" His voice drifted off. "You might be surprised by what you find."

Chapter Nine

The following night, Ben sent a message to Jae. Tenzin had been engaged by Tai to decorate Zhang's banquet hall for Erdun's party, so Ben decided that touring the islands with Jae was a good way to spend the night.

After all, Elder Li had told him to look—*really* look—and he didn't want to ignore the elder's directions.

He met the Jae in the courtyard, wearing a pair of comfortable, wide pants and a thick jacket to cut the winter chill.

"Are you sure you want a tour of the islands?" Jae seemed confused. "You could fly and see them yourself. Nothing is restricted for you. It will be cold, but it's cold on a boat too."

"I'd see them," Ben said, "but I might not understand. You grew up here, didn't you?"

Jae nodded. "I did."

"Then consider yourself my guide." Ben nodded toward the east gate. "I already arranged a boat through Myung. We're meeting it at the Pearl Dock."

Jae seemed to debate himself internally, then sighed. "Very well, but I'm really not sure what it is you want to learn."

"Consider me a curious tourist," Ben said. "I want to know how this world runs." He started walking toward the eastern gate. "How did your meeting with Elder Han go?"

"He's not pleased that we haven't found the seal already, but he was interested to hear what Cheng and Jonathan had to say about Ayal. I believe he has sent a letter to his mate. The messenger is a wind vampire, so it should get to her quickly as long as she's not at sea."

"Good." Ben led Jae through the pathways, nodding to various servants and monks he recognized from his time there. "Mahina might be able to tell us more." Ben glanced at the human. "Have you met her?"

"Mistress Mahina?" Jae nodded. "I had the pleasure of meeting her last year when she was visiting. It was my first opportunity, and I was very impressed with her. She is a tall woman, very broad and powerful with dark curling hair that is very long. Her skin is dark brown, as if she still spends time in the sun." Jae smiled. "An unusual type of vampire for Penglai, but Elder Han will see none above her in wisdom or beauty."

"She sounds formidable."

"She is a *regent*," Jae said. "She takes her duties seriously."

Ben frowned as they walked through the Coral Gate, out the eastern doors, and past the Pearl Gate. The path toward the dock twisted, and seagrass blew across the way, brushing his ankles as he walked with Jae.

"It's curious that she would give up her position in her sire's court to come to Penglai. She has no authority here. No mission. Do you think she just wants a break?"

Jae said, "I wouldn't presume to know her motives. I only know that when she comes, she will be most welcome in Elder Han's household."

They boarded a wide wooden boat with a red sail and a water vampire sitting in the stern. He nodded silently to them and motioned toward the bench in the bow of the ship.

Jae spoke to him in a language Ben didn't recognize, but it sounded like a dialect of Mandarin with a good deal of guttural vocabulary thrown in.

"What language are you speaking?" Ben asked when Jae joined him. "I don't recognize it."

"It's a dialect only spoken on the islands," Jae said. "The original people here were not from the mainland. Now we are a blend of Chinese, Korean, and other ethnic groups."

"Interesting."

The boat took off from the dock and set sail onto a calm, moonlit sea. The waves lapped against the wooden sides, and the breeze came to Ben's fingertips, filling the red sail as they picked up speed.

"We are headed toward the first and smallest of the islands," Jae said. "Kun is hardly more than a port as it is the remnants of a volcano crater. There is a bay along the north side of the island where there is a large fishing town. After we visit that, we can visit Set, which is where I am from. The interior of Set is the best place on the islands to grow wheat."

Ben studied Jae's face to gauge how he felt about his home. "Do you miss it?"

"Miss what?" Jae kept his eyes on the horizon as they sailed toward Kun.

"Living on the island with your family."

"No." Jae shook his head firmly. "Working in an elder's household is the highest honor for any human from the islands. Most humans here never meet an elder even once in their life. I have a brother in the monastery and another who will take over my father's farm. Our parents are very proud of all we are doing." The corner of his mouth turned up. "I'm sure my mother's neighbors likely tire of hearing about her sons."

So Jae's family had a son in the military, one in the church, and one taking over the farm. If that wasn't a feudal story, Ben didn't know what was. "Any sisters?"

"Sadly no." Jae's smile was amused. "Though my brother on the island has married recently, and my mother would love for them to have daughters."

"Do women work on the farms too?"

Jae nodded. "Everyone works. Farming in the traditional way is labor intensive, but it is the healthiest for the people, the land, and the elders."

"Interesting." Was it though? Jae had spoken those lines as if he'd read them from some kind of script. Traditional farming was likely the easiest on the land, yes, but was it really the healthiest for the farmers who worked it? Farming was hard work.

Ben leaned back, watching the peaked shadow in the distance that was quickly growing closer. "Are your grandparents still living?"

"Oh yes," Jae said. "All but my father's father. He died

when I was young, but the rest of my grandparents are healthy and in their eighties now." He smiled. "The island life is the best life. You'll see, Benjamin Vecchio."

———

BEN AND JAE TOURED THE ISLANDS FOR HOURS, MOVING from the bustling fishing village of Kun, which reminded Ben of a historical movie set, to the deep-green wheat fields of Jogé, a long, curving island in the shape of a saber.

Kun was compact and organized, the houses neatly stacked up the hill with glowing gas lamps lighting the cobblestone streets and a noisy tavern that hugged the cliff-side. Bobbing fishing boats rested in the sheltered port, and a Taoist temple sat high at the top of the hill, its gracefully sloped roof outlined in the moonlight.

In Jogé, Ben left the boat and flew over wind-caressed fields of winter wheat and barley, dense stands of evergreen trees, and dotted vegetable patches dark with winter cabbage and root vegetables. Square houses with a combination of thatch and tile roofs dotted the landscape. There appeared to be one main town at the southernmost tip of the island where boats docked to pick up supplies and drop off staples the island couldn't produce, and a single wide road ran up the center of the island, leading to the farms.

Ben saw houses and temples, buffalo, cows, sheep, pigs, and chickens but few structures that looked anything like schools or libraries. There was little evidence of any modern life, no cars, mobile towers, or even radio stations from what he could see. On each island, Jae was quick to point out the medical clinics the elders had set up, but he also was quick to mention that sickness and disease was rare and only the most elderly usually needed a doctor.

Despite the facade of the picturesque, Ben had questions.

Did any of the children get an education on the islands?

Were the islanders allowed to leave if they wanted to?

What about those born with disabilities or chronic health conditions? Were they sent away? Did they simply linger in their family homes until they died?

Ben had studied history and been raised by a five-hundred-year-old vampire; he knew that modern humans often glorified the past without seeing the harshness of the day-to-day reality. There was nothing romantic about living without modern plumbing and health care.

Jae showed him all the islands that stretched from Penglai in the southwest up to Jogé at the northeast corner. The fishing island Kun, the verdant isle of Set, and Male made up the rest of the chain. Kun and Male were mainly fishing islands while Set and Jogé were cultivated for crops. In total, Jae estimated that around five thousand humans lived on all five islands.

They were sailing back to Penglai, and Ben had more and more questions swirling in his mind, but he didn't want to offend Jae, who seemed nothing but proud of the island way of life. Ben could see many advantages. The people lived an active, satisfying life where the elders provided everything they needed that they could not produce themselves, and in turn, they provided the elders with food, fish, and tradable goods that could keep the islands in balance.

And blood. Ben couldn't forget the blood.

According to Jae, all islanders understood that some of their number would be taken to the main island every week as part of the blood-stock for the vampires on Penglai. There was no preserved blood on Penglai Island, and blood-wine was rare. Humans were the only source of food, and while Ben knew that all the monks and most of the residents were provided to the vampires as blood donors, he hadn't really put together that those humans on the islands might not have a choice in the matter.

———

BEN WAS SITTING IN THEIR SLEEPING QUARTERS, writing notes in a journal, when Tenzin finally returned from decorating the banquet hall.

"I have folded so many paper flowers tonight, I think my hands might be sore." She looked at them in confusion. "I can't remember the last time my hands were sore."

Ben turned and looked at her. "Do you remember what sore really feels like?"

"Not really, but I know it's not pleasant."

"It comes from your muscles being inflamed from overuse."

She frowned. "I can't be sore then." Vampire muscles could be cut, could be bruised, could even be torn, but they couldn't really be overused. "Whatever the feeling is, it is not pleasant."

She was tiny and indignant, but she was also beautiful.

"Tenzin?"

"Hmm?" She was staring at her fingertips. "I think my fingers were cut many times."

"Paper cuts. Have you been to the outer islands?"

"What are paper cuts? And no, not for years." She looked up. "Why would I go to the outer islands?"

"To see how the islanders live."

"But that hasn't changed in hundreds of years." She walked to the bathroom and returned with a damp cloth that she put over her hands. "That feels better."

"The islanders' lives haven't changed in hundreds of years," Ben repeated. "Think about that."

She looked up. "What is to think about? Life here at Penglai hasn't changed either. I realize you miss your mobile devices here, but there is a phone room—"

"It's not my mobile phone I'm talking about." Ben walked over to her. "I'm talking about basic things, Tenzin. Plumbing. Schools. Electricity. Most of the islands don't even have electricity."

"So they go to bed when the sun goes down." Tenzin shrugged. "I don't understand what—"

"Are they prisoners here?"

She froze. "That's... complicated."

"Why?"

"Because technically these islands don't exist. Not to any human government. Not in the modern world. Therefore, the people who live here—according to the outside world—don't exist either."

He wasn't surprised. "So if someone wanted to leave?"

"Why would they?" She frowned. "Humans on the islands work hard, yes. But they also never suffer hunger or war or homelessness. There are no drugs here. Alcohol exists, but the abuse of it does not."

Ben crossed his arms. "Why not?"

"You *want* there to be alcohol abuse?" Her eyebrows went up.

"No, but I want humans to have free will." He kept his eyes on her. "And I don't think it really exists here. What would happen if someone was unhappy and started abusing alcohol in the town?"

"One of the vampire administrators would take them, use amnis, and make sure they didn't abuse alcohol in the future."

"And you think that's right?" Ben wasn't shocked, but he was. "They're taking their free will away."

"It would be better for that person's family and community to suffer their abuse?" Tenzin was confused. "What are you saying? That that single individual's bad choices are more valuable than the good of the whole community?"

Wait, *was* that what he was saying? Ben shook his head. "I'm talking about free will, Tenzin."

"And I'm talking about safety and responsibility." Tenzin frowned. "They're *humans*. If they're going to live together peacefully, they need rules."

"And vampires don't need rules?"

"Vampires have more rules than humans by far," Tenzin said. "We have hierarchies and tribute and sires and offspring and allies. There are rules governing every one of those relationships."

He didn't deny that, but there was still something about the islands that didn't sit right with him. Were most of the islanders happy? Probably.

But what if some of them weren't?

Tenzin walked over and put her hand on his cheek. "Don't put modern morality or ideas onto a place that hasn't moved in centuries, Ben. It just doesn't fit." She stood on her tiptoes and kissed his lips gently. "The people here are happy, content, and are provided with everything they need. Can you say the same about most humans in the modern world?"

"No," he admitted. "Not even a little bit."

"So I'm right." She looked at her hands. "Paper cuts would make an effective torture device. Not that I torture people anymore, but should the need arise..."

Something about the islands of Penglai still sat uneasily in Ben's chest, and he felt a burst of irritation with his mate, who had shoved the quality of human life on the islands out of her mind so she could focus on paper cuts.

"I'm going out for a walk." He stood and abruptly left their chamber. "I'll be back before dawn."

Chapter Ten

They met with Zhang at dusk the following night. Tenzin appeared nonplussed about seeing her sire, but there was a low hum of tension through their shared amnis that she couldn't hide.

They hadn't spoken much that morning. In the predawn light, Ben had watched the monks in the garden moving silently about their chores, sweeping pathways, trimming bushes, and clearing a dusting of snow from the steps around the great hall.

They all seemed content, but how would he know if they weren't? Their order existed to serve the Eight Immortals, who were venerated almost as gods to the devout on the islands.

Or so he'd been told.

"Benjamin." Zhang greeted Ben warmly when they arrived in his personal lounge. Low couches were propped up along the walls of a small room with an open section in the center of the roof. Below the opening, a fire glowed in a brass brazier that heated the sitting area to a comfortable temperature. Before they sat, a monk silently stole into the room and added several pieces of glowing charcoal, then slipped away without a word from either Zhang or the monk.

"Please." Zhang motioned to the seats across from him. "Join me. Tai is bringing blood."

Tenzin slid in first; then Ben followed.

His mate stared at Zhang from across the glowing brazier. "I don't like that you roped us into this. There's some kind of subterfuge going on with the Pearl Seal, and you haven't told us what it is yet."

Zhang said nothing, just waited as Tai entered the room, set out three goblets, and poured fresh blood into them.

Ben couldn't help thinking of whatever poor island resident had bled into his cup. Was it a man? A woman? Maybe even one of the teenagers he'd seen working alongside the adults? Had the person ever met a vampire? Did they know what their blood was helping to sustain? Were they happy or were the islands a prison the donor wanted to escape?

"Thanks to those who sacrificed for this sustenance," Zhang muttered before he drained his goblet in one long draft. "Ben, aren't you hungry?"

Ben took his blood and finished it quickly, but Tenzin only sat and watched her sire with narrowed eyes.

"The Pearl Seal," she said. "What is going on?"

Zhang's eyebrows rose in silent amusement. "Would you believe that I don't know?"

"No," Tenzin said.

"Yes." Ben looked at her. "I keep telling you this isn't some grand conspiracy. I think someone stole it for the gold."

Zhang lifted one finger. "There I disagree with you, Benjamin. Anyone who stole the seal to make money would need a buyer in the outside world or a broker to sell it for him or her. Most people here on the island don't know how to use a telephone, much less engineer a sophisticated art heist. Remember who you're dealing with."

The answer should have satisfied Ben because it made sense, but there was something that didn't sit right with him.

"Does this have to do with a shift in power?" Tenzin asked. "Will Mahina's arrival throw off the current balance? Is that why someone doesn't want her to settle here?"

Zhang didn't answer immediately, which led Ben to think Tenzin was onto something.

"Mahina is a regent," Ben said. "Jae was very clear about that, which means that Elder Han has been clear with his household that they are to treat her as his equal."

"She's also the daughter of an ancient," Tenzin said. "Sina is your elder by how many years? No one knows. She could be as Saba in the sea, and Mahina is her most beloved child."

"But not her only," Zhang said. "Sina had many children."

"Still," Ben said. "Could one of the elders here resent the idea of that concentration of power in Han's camp?"

"Lu Dongbin," Tenzin said.

"No." Zhang shook his head firmly.

"Just because he's your oldest friend and ally doesn't mean he's incapable of political machinations," Tenzin said. "In fact, it makes him far more likely to protect his power as the other water vampire on the council."

"Elder Han represents the southern territories, and Elder Lu the north," Ben said. "Isn't that right?"

"Now a powerful vampire of the south sea is joining her mate in Penglai," Tenzin said.

Zhang held up a hand. "I understand your reasoning, but it is false." He leaned closer and dropped his voice to barely over a whisper. "Privately, Elder Lu is in favor of a reinforcement of our southern waters. Between Cheng and Sina's mate, an extra southern ballast is welcome." Zhang turned his attention to Ben. "I understand you put on quite the display for Cheng's people."

Ben blinked. "How did you know—?"

"I have my sources in his company," Zhang said. "They were impressed. Well done. It was subtle but a formidable display of power."

So that was another pat on the back for a gross display of jealousy and power. Ben was really batting a thousand with the neolithic-justice crowd on this trip.

"We'll keep working on it," Tenzin said. "Ben toured the islands last night. He's worried about the children going to school."

"The island children go to school," Zhang said. "I believe it is mandatory for both girls and boys though grade six."

"What about college?"

Zhang shrugged. "They don't need college to do their work. Reading, writing, mathematics, and simple history of the islands is enough for the work they do."

"But what if they want to do other work? What if they want to be a... scientist? Or an artist?"

"We have an artists' guild," Zhang said. "Who do you

think paints the murals that decorate our rooms here? Who carves the screens or works the metal?" Zhang appeared amused. "You have a very modern perspective, Benjamin, which is expected. But education can come in many forms. Not everyone needs a Western university degree to excel in life."

Ben hardly thought any of the islanders were given the chance to excel, but he kept his mouth shut. This wasn't his home. These weren't his people. He'd only be feeding into stereotypes about Western superiority if he criticized Penglai's way of life.

"I give in." He raised his hands. "Life on the islands is idyllic, and the humans here want for nothing."

Zhang smiled. "Life can be hard everywhere," he said. "This year we were informed the wheat crop was low. Luckily, we can bring in wheat from the outside world. If we did not, many of our residents might go hungry this winter."

"Huh." Ben was impressed. "If that was a small wheat crop, I should come back in a good year and see a big one. The farming islands are incredibly lush even in winter. I enjoyed my tour with Jae."

Tenzin and Zhang exchanged a look but said nothing, leaving Ben with the feeling, once again, that he'd been left out of something important.

———

"I don't want to talk about it."

Ben stormed through the outer garden as workers bustled around them, fetching greenery, sweeping pathways, and hoisting ladders with the assistance of a few helpful wind vampires.

"But why are you angry?"

He stopped and turned. Tenzin nearly floated into him.

"I'm not," he said. "I just want to meet with Jae and touch base. Have a drink." He glanced over his shoulder. "You told Tai you'd help with the preparations for Mahina's arrival, right?"

"Yes." Tenzin narrowed her eyes.

"So you do that, and I'll get with Jae. He said he wants to go over the work details for all the humans doing restoration on the seal the week before it went missing. Two sets of eyes will be more than enough for that."

He sounded so reasonable, but Tenzin felt a low buzz of irritation growing in her amnis, and she didn't know if it was her own anger or Ben's.

Maybe it was both.

"Fine." She didn't wait for her mate to say another word; she simply flew up and over the bustling outer garden and away from Ben.

Once, Tenzin had battled the twin urges in her blood to destroy anything that might keep her apart from Benjamin while also experiencing the occasional impulse to eliminate him because he was a weakness and a distraction.

Nothing about becoming his mate had conquered those dueling desires. If anything, her longing for him became more intense, as did the instinct to strangle him as he slept.

She wouldn't, because it would be akin to strangling herself—and she was nothing if not a survivor—but when her mate said one thing with his mouth and another with his actions, she was tempted to make him bleed.

Just a little.

Instead, she let him walk down to the tavern with Jae to look over human paperwork that would tell them nothing.

There was something else she needed to investigate, but she couldn't formulate her thoughts into anything concrete yet. She only had an itching suspicion at the back of her mind that didn't warrant exploration unless she could see some things for herself.

"Tenzin?"

She turned and saw Tai waving at her, so she walked over. "I may not be able to assist you tonight."

"It's fine," he said. "We accomplished what I wanted for the party preparations last night, but I was curious if you were committed to the investigation tonight."

"In a manner of speaking, yes."

"Ah." Tai nodded. "Then I shall recruit one of Elder Zhongli's household to assist me."

"What's going on?"

"We received word from Sina's court that their party is three nights away," Tai said. "Normally preparations only go on during the day and out of sight of the elders, but with this short notice, we must work at night too. There are some roof tiles that need to be replaced in the palace, and it's far more efficient if the wind vampires replace them instead of having humans stumbling all over the roofs."

"That makes sense." She felt torn. "If I finish early tonight, I will check with you."

Tai bowed. "Of course, but don't rush your work. I'm sure

we will have more than enough time to finish with the help of Elder Zhongli's household."

Tenzin supposed part of this shortfall was her own fault since she'd been the one to kill all of Zhang's rotten spawn thousands of years ago. If she hadn't, they likely would have sired half-decent workers for Zhang's household now.

Then again, what's done was done. She was never one to dwell in the past. "I'll check with you before dawn."

Tai waved and Tenzin flew off, creating a bubble of air around herself to shield her body from the frigid winter wind across the Bohai Sea.

As she left the shores of Penglai and flew north over the sheer face of the mountain where the palace was situated, she looked down at the cliff that met the ocean and saw white-caps of ice beating against the rocky north side of the sacred island.

She flew through the ever-present bank of fog that water vampires carefully built to shield the island from outsider view and skipped the familiar and friendly lights of Kun to her right before heading north to the island of Set.

She made it in a little over thirty minutes and landed on the highest point of the island where a Taoist temple stood. Someone had cast a massive bell to serve as both a meditation and a call to the residents of the island if gathering was necessary. Its dark bronze surface was frosted over with a sheen of ice, and sharp wind whipped the cedars and pines that surrounded the temple.

Tenzin surveyed the island, noting the gentle slopes that tumbled down from the high point of the temple. Foothills really, the rolling hills of Set were covered with waving green fields of wheat and barley, the two grain staples of the islands. While some islanders enjoyed the imported rice from the mainland, the islands weren't suitable places to grow rice, the climate too unforgiving for the warm-weather crop.

She floated over the hills and gentle valleys of Set, noting the abundance of thriving crops, the huddled livestock in the trees, and the deep green leaves of winter vegetables.

After she examined Set, she flew north, veering off to the east to catch the edge of Male before she hit the southern tip of Jogé.

There she saw the same abundance she saw on the island of Set. There were thriving fields of burgeoning grain that would be more than enough to feed the islands when they were ready to harvest in the spring. Added to that, the storehouses on the islands seemed to be full of corn and potatoes from the summer planting, and there was no lack of livestock, no hungry-looking animals.

The islands of Penglai appeared to be thriving, as ready to sustain the long winter as they ever were. Good news for the islands, the elders, and the daoshi who served them.

So why was the harbormaster of Penglai town importing wheat and other staples from the mainland?

Chapter Eleven

He unwrapped the stolen seal only during the daytime. Unlike most places, the most secret time on the islands was not in the dead of night but when the sun was high and shadows were thin on the ground.

He locked his door, closed the wooden shutters, and rolled down the heavy wool blankets that kept the cold from stealing into his small house. Then he spread out the woolen blanket that had once been his wife's favorite on cold nights.

He couldn't bring himself to look directly at the dragon's eye, so he focused on the jade fish swimming across the bright orange flowers that Shuang had loved so much; the edge of the blanket was edged in bright yellow satin.

Put her on the blanket, Xīngān. Look at her sweet face. She is so perfect. I'm going to draw a picture.

He still had Shuang's sketches, all of them stored in a box near the corner shrine where he and his daughter lit candles on Shuang's birthday. His wife had not wanted them to remember the day she died.

Remember me on my birthday, Xīngān. Remember me on the day I started living, not the day I stopped.

She had been everything to him. His own heart. For days after her death, the women in the village brought food for Tianyu and the small silent girl that pretty, bright Shuang had left behind. His wife had been everyone's friend, but now her small family lived in isolation and her husband was a thief.

A thief.

What have you done, Tianyu?

Her memory accused him.

Surely you must know, Shuang. You, her mother, will understand that I did this for her.

Shuang's daughter deserved so much more than her mother's fate. He knew there was more in the outside world. He had heard stories about others like Jiayi and knew their daughter was not facing judgment from a past life or the anger of the gods. She was too bright, too cheerful, despite the misunderstanding of others.

His daughter was brilliant and kind, gifted in ways her humble father couldn't understand. There hadn't been a day that had passed since Shuang had died that he didn't wish his wife could see their daughter and what she could create.

The eye of the dragon accused him. *Thief. What success can come to the daughter of a thief?*

But surely others were more corrupt than he. After all, Tianyu had not been the one to think of this scheme, only the one with the skills to remove the seal without doing the delicate artifact any harm. Surely the gods would judge others more harshly than him and allow Shuang's daughter a gentler path.

All he wanted was what had been promised. He wanted the accusing dragon away from its hiding place under the bed and in someone else's hands. He wanted passage off the island with Jiayi and the papers they were promised. He had maps and pictures of the giant machines called railways. He could get his daughter to Shanghai, and from there?

Tianyu would find a way. With the money from the seal, they would be able to—

A tap at the door, and he hastily wrapped the Pearl Seal back in Shuang's blanket, sending a prayer to his wife to ask the dragon for favor and forgiveness.

He slid the blanket under his bed, then opened the door to see his daughter's round face smudged with bright colors from the paints she was using in her latest work.

Jiayi motioned with her hands in the special language they had created for each other.

I'm hungry.

He motioned back. *Noodles?*

She shook her head, then curved her hands together with a grin.

He copied her motions and rolled his eyes. *Dumplings? Again?*

His daughter's cheeks reminded him of two soft dumplings, the dimples marking her as Shuang's daughter, though she had traces of his own features too. Luckily, she looked more like her mother.

Yes. He nodded. *I'll go out. Dumplings.*

She danced back into the main room of the house and toward her paints.

He walked out of his bedroom and donned the heavy quilted jacket that hung over the bookcase with Shuang's books.

Tianyu had tried to teach their daughter to read and write without much success. He was not a teacher, and Jiayi wasn't allowed to attend the village school as she was. Jiayi knew a few things, enough that he could send her to the shops with a list if she felt brave enough to weather the stares of others in the town.

He walked out with a pocket full of coins—his monthly portion from the elders was generous, more than enough to support a wife and daughter, so he and Jiayi never lacked for food or any other small luxuries Penglai town offered. Things like the satin-lined blanket from the mainland were out of reach for many artisans on the island who couldn't waste money on imported blankets.

Tianyu nodded at shopkeepers and other craftsmen and women as he passed through the cobbled streets of Penglai. Most of the town on the main island was full of workers like him, the wealthier farmers and fishermen having large houses and property on the outer islands.

He reached the dumpling shop where Jiayi's favorite pork buns were almost sold out. He only saw a few in the window, so he tapped and grabbed the attention of Mistress Fang, who opened the window with a smile that nearly matched Jiayi's.

"Back again, Tianyu?"

"She can't get enough of them," he said. "I think she is

going to turn into a dumpling one day."

Mistress Fang chuckled. "She has good taste; I can't argue with her. I'll put in a few extra with the leeks too. Tell her they're good when it's cold outside." Mistress Fang's smile fell. "Can she understand that kind of thing?"

No one knew why Shuang's daughter could not speak or hear, though most believed it must have been the same reason her mother had wasted away from illness. Fate had decided the path of their current lives must be harder to balance out something in the past.

He dearly wished he knew what phenomenal fortune they had squandered in another life that had left him without a wife and his daughter without hearing or a voice.

"Of course she understands." He nodded. "I'll tell her."

"And tell Jiayi that I hung her drawing of the shop in a frame. Look!" Mistress Fang motioned behind her to where a pencil drawing had been framed and hung in a place of pride. "When she wants to, she should come see it. People ask me all the time who drew such a good picture, and most of them don't believe me when I say she's only seven."

His heart filled with pride. Mistress Fang was one of the few in Penglai town who didn't treat Jiayi as if she were a broken or cursed child. "Thank you, mistress. I'll tell her; she'll be so pleased."

He paid for the bag of dumplings, then started back to his house, thinking of how happy Jiayi would be if she saw her drawing hanging proudly at the dumpling shop.

"Ho there!" Haitao, a harness maker he'd been waiting on for over a week now, flagged him down. "Tianyu, you haven't been bothering me these days. Did something more important catch your attention?" Haitao's eyes glittered with some secret.

Tianyu schooled his face. The harness maker knew nothing. He was only a harness maker after all. What could he know of Tianyu or the terrible bargain he'd had to make?

"Just busy at the palace with all the renovations," Tianyu said. "Is my harness ready?" He'd been without his horse cart for days because his harness had broken. Tianyu was tired of walking around the island with all his carpentry gear or hiring a cart for the day. He wanted his horse and cart useful again.

"It's ready, yes." Haitao stepped closer. "But the price has gone up, my friend."

Tianyu frowned. "What are you talking about? We already agreed on a fair price. Should I report you to the magistrate for trying to cheat me? What would the elders say?"

"Oh, I don't think you want to report me to the magistrate, my friend." He lowered his voice. "After all, you wouldn't want Myung to know what you have hidden in your house, would you?"

Tianyu's jacket couldn't keep out the cold that trickled down his neck when he heard Haitao's words. "I don't know what you're talking about."

"I'm not dumb like your little girl." The man's eyes gleamed with greed. "And I don't think you want to test me, or this harness might get more and more expensive every day."

———

Tenzin watched Ben as he entered the room, wary of his mood and waiting to see what he said first.

"Well, we went over and over the work records, but there was nothing unusual about the weeks leading up to the theft." He set down a pile of papers. "I brought a copy of the records if you want to look at them, but I can't see anything that stands out. The most notable thing in there is the day a harness broke on a horse cart when a carpenter was driving back to Penglai town on the Pearl Gate road." Ben sat down and ran a hand through his hair. "He had to load his equipment on the mason's cart and a bunch of lacquer spilled."

She flew over, still wary. "That sounds annoying."

"The gardeners weren't happy."

"About the horse cart?"

"About the lacquer. It's not good for the soil."

"No, it wouldn't be."

She hovered across from him, still trying to gauge his mood.

"What is with you?" His mood was annoyed now.

The question made no sense. "What do you think is with me?"

"I don't know, but you and Zhang were doing the whole 'let's have secrets we don't tell Ben' thing earlier tonight, and now you're floating over there like you're trying to read me and I hate that."

"I know you hate that."

"So why do you do it?" Now his mood was exasperated.

"Because I'm still learning how to read you, and since we have this... blood bond, it's hard for me to tell what are my own feelings and what are yours. And Zhang and I were not keeping secrets."

"Yeah, you definitely were." His eyes had relaxed, and he didn't appear as annoyed as he had been. "I have trouble with that too, you know."

"Keeping secrets with Zhang?"

"No. Sorting my feelings out from yours."

"Oh." She let her feet touch the ground. "I don't like it."

"That doesn't surprise me. What were you and Zhang hiding earlier?"

She sighed. "We weren't hiding anything. I had a thought, and I think he had a similar thought, but it was more of a question than a thought, and now I have discovered some answers but I have even more questions."

Ben blinked and appeared confused. "Give me a second... You had a thought that was a question?"

"Yes."

He frowned. "So you answered that question, but now you have more questions?"

"There's more than enough wheat on the islands. We were told there was a shortage, which is why they had to order wheat, remember? But I flew over the islands tonight, and the harvest should be very good unless there are storms that are unseasonably cold, which there shouldn't be because my father redirects any severe storms when it's necessary."

Ben blinked. "Zhang can...? Never mind. So I was right? There isn't a food shortage."

"Unless there was a poor harvest last year, there shouldn't be, which is why I have more questions," Tenzin said. "Why is Myung ordering grain from the mainland? Are the farmers telling him their crops are bad? Why would they do that? Is Myung trying to cheat the elders? That would be extremely stupid and dangerous; I hardly think he'd endanger his position for the cost of some wheat."

"Right." Ben nodded. "So the thought you had with Zhang was the question about the wheat, which you answered, but now you have more questions."

"Exactly. You mentioned that the wheat looked good to you when we met with Zhang earlier. You're not a farmer, but I think Zhang and I had the same thought—was there really a shortage?—which is why we had the look that you thought was hiding something, but we weren't hiding anything. We just didn't share the thought aloud."

"Why not?"

Tenzin opened her mouth to respond but found that she didn't have an answer. "I don't know."

Ben pulled Tenzin to sit on his lap. "I do."

"Then why did you ask me if I knew?"

"Because I wanted to know if you were aware of it or if it's just something that you do out of habit."

She nodded. "That is a good reason."

"You and Zhang are both secretive by nature." Ben started running a hand up and down her back. It felt delightful, and she didn't want to listen to what he was saying. She wanted to focus on his hand.

But she knew he wanted her to focus on what he was saying, so she tried to ignore the hand.

"It's been just the two of you here for thousands of years." His hand slowed around the small of her back and started rubbing small circles at the base of her spine.

Tenzin felt her eyes crossing, and she had the urge to bite his arm to keep him from distracting her. "Yes?"

"When it's just the two of you, you have a way of communicating that leaves everyone else out. It's not conscious, but it's habit for you both." His fingers splayed and pressed in, his amnis dancing along the skin bared by the edge of her shirt. "You don't mean to do it, but you often leave me out of your reasoning or thinking on something because I can't read all those minute facial cues the two of you have."

"Hmmm." She breathed out. "You're right. We need to work on communicating more effectively with you. It's not intentional."

"I realized that about halfway through tonight, but I still wanted to torment you a little bit for pissing me off."

She let her head fall forward. "So this extensive lecture while you're rubbing my back—"

"Is completely designed to drive you crazy." His hand slid inside the back of her leggings and cupped her bottom. "I know you have trouble thinking when you're physically aroused."

She swung her leg over and straddled his legs. "I'm both irritated and impressed."

"And it turns you on."

"So much." She bent down and captured his lips with her mouth, cutting his lip with her fang and sucking the rounded curve of his lower lip into her mouth. "Enough talking for tonight."

He stood and held her up with his arms and his element. "I can agree to that."

Chapter Twelve

For their next meeting with Jae, Ben requested that they meet in Elder Han's offices near the great hall instead of at the tavern in Penglai town.

"If Myung is involved" —he and Tenzin were walking across the grounds of the palace— "it's very likely he has spies in the village."

"We need to know how the business of the island is run," Tenzin said. "How is the grain counted? Who keeps track?"

"It seems to me that Myung has a lot of power, maybe more than we even know. He's the harbormaster to the islands, which means he controls who comes and goes. For isolated humans like the ones here on the islands, he's maybe even more powerful than the elders."

Tenzin frowned. "I hadn't thought of that before, but you're right."

They arrived at Elder Han's administrative offices, where half a dozen clerks were busy in the business of the day-to-day administration of vast territories.

Ben suspected it was much like what Zhang's clerks did. Lots of letter writing, answering messengers who arrived in person, tabulating tribute from various vampire leaders on the mainland, and more.

The Eight Immortals ruled the mainland of Eastern Asia from the southern tip that dipped into the South China Sea to the peak of Kongur Tagh in the west and the curving depths of Lake Baikal in the north. Within those stretches, four of the Eight administered the northern territories and the other four, the southern lands.

Within each territory were hundreds of local vampires, heads of clans, and other chiefs whose bands of immortals looked to them for authority, but each of those minor heads—unless they wanted to defy empire and tradition—owed tribute and authority to one of the Eight Immortals.

Conflicts were handled locally, but if agreement could not be reached, a counselor was secured. If that counselor could not come to a suitable agreement with the parties in conflict, a minister was called for, and if they could not find a solution, a magistrate was summoned. All of these positions were administered and watched over by the elders and their staff of bureaucrats. Only the most severe conflicts were ever brought to the great hall, but hundreds of letters poured in every month, asking for favor, petitioning for reprieve, or making other requests within the jurisdiction of the palace.

It was a complex system that had nonetheless worked for thousands of years, making the Eight Immortals of Penglai Island the vastest and most stable empire in the vampire world. Ben's mind had been blown when Tai introduced him to Zhang's head clerk, who oversaw a dozen others who themselves were the heads for a hundred more in other parts of the territory.

It was modern feudalism on a vast scale, but somehow it worked. Ben had always surmised that for vampires—who valued age, wealth, and power over any shared moral code—a relatively benevolent dictatorship was probably the most workable way to govern.

He spotted Jae across the office and waved at him. "There he is."

Tenzin saw the clerks watching them with suspicion. "Hopefully there's a private room where we can meet."

Jae pointed to the right, and they headed toward a dark wooden door. When they walked through it, Jae followed, closing the door behind him.

"I've ordered tea." He motioned to a pair of low sofas in an alcove near a trickling fountain. "I try not to bother the clerks here; they're always so busy."

"Is that why you prefer meeting at the tavern?" Tenzin asked.

"Yes." He nodded. "I also like being among humans. Please don't take offense, but I'm often the only human at the table when I meet within the palace. It can be unnerving."

"I used to be the same way," Ben said. "No offense taken. We asked you to meet here at the palace because we have some questions about Myung."

Jae's eyebrows went up. "Do you? He's a water vampire. The son of Elder Lu, who is a close ally of your sire of course."

"Of course," Tenzin said. "How long has he been the harbormaster of Penglai town?"

Jae frowned. "I think you would know far better than me, Tenzin. Long before I was born, I assume."

"Right." Tenzin fell quiet as a servant entered the room with a tea tray.

Jae motioned for the servant to leave after he'd set the tray down; then Jae served Ben and Tenzin two steaming cups of jasmine-scented tea.

"We usually come by air," Ben said. "So you can imagine we're not overly familiar with the comings and goings of the ships in the harbor. I was only on one once, the first time I came, save for the yacht we took down to Cheng's place in Shanghai."

"Of course." Jae frowned. "Why are you asking about Myung? Do you think he had something to do with the theft of the Pearl Seal?"

Ben glanced at Tenzin, curious how much she would want to share with Jae.

"No," she said. "There was something else that caught my attention, having to do with the grain harvest. Purely a curiosity, but I remember that your father is a grain farmer. Does Myung run the storehouses on the island? He mentioned needing to import grain, and I was curious where it was coming from."

"For that you would do better asking one of the heads of house," Jae said. "I confess that even though my father grew the grain, I never paid much attention to it after the harvesters brought it in." Jae smiled. "I concentrate on security matters, not where the bakers get their flour."

Tenzin nodded. "Very well. Speaking of security, Ben mentioned that you went over the work records from the work on the Pearl Gate repairs a few weeks ago. Where did you get the records?"

Jae said, "From Myung's clerks. His office in Penglai town is in charge of assigning workers to jobs from the palace offices."

"So something needs to be done in the palace," Ben said. "A door is broken or a flagstone needs to be replaced. The palace sends a work request to Myung's office, and he's the one who chooses the worker for the job?"

Jae nodded. "That's correct."

Tenzin looked at Ben and this time, he could read her expression clearly.

They really needed to talk with Myung.

———

INSTEAD, THEIR NEXT MEETING WAS WITH TAI.

"Grain?" The vampire frowned as he directed servants to move chairs in Zhang's banquet hall for the party. "Why are you asking about grain?"

"Because it's become a point of interest," Tenzin said, not elaborating further. "Vampires all eat a little bit to keep their stomachs from aching, and the food of choice is—"

"Noodle soup," Zhang's household manager said. "Yes, the chefs in each household make their own versions, depending on the taste of the elder. I believe our chefs here favor a recipe using mutton and wide noodles. Why are you asking about grain?" Tai asked again.

"Where do the chefs get the grain on the island?" Ben asked.

"From the monastery. They're the ones who mill the barley and wheat into flour, then package it and deliver it to the palace, the town, and the outer islands. They also store the rice we import for some of the southern vampires who prefer it."

"So the grain is kept at the monastery?"

Tai frowned. "I believe so. It's one of their chief duties, keeping track of food stores on the island. Each of the islands has their own fresh markets, but all grain—the wheat, the corn, and the barley—is collected and kept at the monastery. Partly to make sure it's distributed fairly and partly because that's where the grain mill is."

Ben asked, "Would it be possible for us to meet with the head of the monastery?"

Tai narrowed his eyes. "Does this have something to do with the theft?"

"Probably not," Tenzin said. "Can we meet him?"

"Her," Tai said. "And yes, I will arrange a meeting for you in two nights."

Ben balked. "It'll take that long to see her?"

"No," Tai said. "But Erdun's party is tomorrow night, and Mistress Mahina is arriving the night after that, and while you two don't enjoy diplomatic affairs and honorary receptions, as Elder Zhang's only children, you'll need to be at both. But I should be able to take you to see her before Mistress Mahina is received." He turned back to the servants who were waiting with low tables stacked in a corner. "And bring Erdun a present. He likes sweet aaruul, the drier the better. You'll have time to get it if you leave for the mainland in the next hour."

Tai walked away, and Ben turned to Tenzin. "What is aaruul?"

Her face was scrunched up in distaste. "You never got to experience aaruul in Khentii?"

"Not that I remember."

"It's a sour milk curd cheese that's dried until it feels like rocks in your mouth." She looked at him. "Sometimes they make it with sugar and fruit, and Erdun loves it. There's a lady in Beijing who makes it, but we'll probably need to break into her shop to get it before tomorrow night."

"We're breaking into a shop in Beijing to steal dry cheese?"

"It's kind of like candy, okay? For some people." She pulled his arm and headed back to their chambers. "Let's put on an extra layer. It's snowing outside."

———

TENZIN WAS HALFWAY DOWN THE VENTILATION SHAFT when she realized she'd made a mistake.

"Shit."

She smelled the dog before she could see it, but if there was a dog below her, that would mean there would be barking, which meant there would be noise, and the old woman who ran the Mongolian grocery in the Miyun District in North Beijing would wake from her small apartment above the store.

She should have remembered that Mongolians were far more likely to keep dogs than the average Chinese resident.

"What's wrong?" Ben asked above her.

"There may be barking."

"There's a dog?"

"I smell one."

"If it's one of those massive bankhars, I may hurt you, Tenzin. One of those things almost bit off my foot when I came too close to a sheep one time. I didn't even know dogs could move that fast."

"It's probably something small." It smelled like a mastiff, but she wasn't going to tell Ben that. "We'll just keep to the top of the room."

She floated down the shaft and could already hear a low growl coming from the throat of the dog she'd smelled.

Okay, it wasn't a small dog. As she removed the air-intake cover, she saw the hulking beast sitting in a corner of the shop, staring at her as she set the metal cover gently on the top of a store shelf.

"It's not a small dog," Tenzin said. "But it's not... huge."

She'd seen Tibetan mastiffs that were bigger. Barely.

This dog was black with brown markings around the eyes and a curled tail that quivered as it watched her. She slid into the room, keeping her back to the ceiling and floating over colorful shelves of dried goods, canned meat, and liquor bottles.

"Holy shit, he's looking right at us." Ben finally made it into the shop. "How high do you think he can jump?"

"Not twelve feet," Tenzin said. Probably. She'd seen a bankhar dog take down an eagle once. It was intimidating. "I see the aaruul."

"If we end up losing any body parts to get Erdun sour-cheese candy, I'm going to be so pissed off," Ben said. "Tenzin, grab the stuff and let's go."

"Distract him," she said. "The aaruul is on the lowest shelf by the register."

"Are you kidding me?" He did not sound pleased.

"Probably to tempt the kids when their mothers are checking out," Tenzin said. "Who can resist aaruul?"

"I'm distracting him. Grab the stuff and go."

She inched over to the counter, eyeing the bright red wrappers on the child-size packages. Just as she was sinking down to grab a box of the candies, she spotted a yellow-and-purple flower that appeared to be homemade aaruul behind a glass counter.

"Keep distracting him; I spotted the good stuff."

"Can we maybe assume that Erdun's not going to be super picky about this stuff and just grab what's easy?" Ben hissed, "He's moving. He's coming toward me, Tenzin."

The sound of growling got louder. Apparently the dog wasn't happy that Ben hadn't left yet even though he was just floating near the ceiling.

"Can you use amnis on dogs?" Ben asked.

"I've never tried." Tenzin reached into the glass display and pinched a pressed aaruul candy, glad to see that it was nicely dried. She quickly stuffed a dozen of the round flowers into a paper bag.

"Tenzin, he's climbing on the shelves."

"He can't climb shelves—he's a dog."

The growling had turned from a low rumble into an audible snarl.

"Toss a shoe at him or something," she said. "Distract him. Dogs like shoes."

"I'm wearing leather Velascas!"

"I'm sure the dog won't care."

He muttered low curses in Italian.

She heard something hard hit the ground, and she grabbed another dozen aaruul flowers just to be safe. After all, it was Erdun's hundredth birthday.

"That didn't work, and he is climbing on boxes, Tenzin!"

She rolled her eyes. "I'm coming."

Tenzin stuffed the aaruul in her jacket, tossed a gold coin on the counter, then swiftly flew over to the boxes where the dog had reached a truly impressive height in his attempt to reach Benjamin, who was only a few feet away, now with one foot clad only in a sock.

She tugged on the dog's ear, startling it and causing the box to collapse beneath the animal, who fell to the floor, barking furiously at the intruders in his mistress's shop.

"Come *on!*" Ben nearly shoved her up the ventilation shaft before he followed her.

Tenzin was laughing when she reached the roof, flying into the frosty night as Ben raced behind her. She darted between the darkened buildings of the Chinese capital, dipping low to skim over the expressways and weaving through the heights of the massive apartment buildings that littered the metropolis.

Ben chased her, and she could feel his rueful delight through their mating bond. He was trying to stay grumpy, but he was having too much fun. She twisted in the sky, enjoying the sheer power of speed, the whipping winter wind that rushed off the northern mountains, and the chill of the salt air as she headed toward the open sea.

Ben caught her foot just as she was heading south over the water.

"Tiny!"

She turned around and saw that he was pointing to the east. The sun was starting to glow on the horizon; she hadn't realized the trip to the mainland had taken so long.

She waved at him, then headed north. She knew of a bayside holiday resort that would be nearly empty this time of year.

By the time the sun rose, Ben and Tenzin were ensconced in an abandoned bungalow with winter waves crashing in the distance, and her mate was drifting off to sleep.

"So you got it, right?" His voice was a drowsy murmur.

Tenzin pulled the paper bag from her jacket. "I did."

"Good." His eyes fluttered. "I hope it was worth it, because you now owe me... a very expensive... pair of shoes."

Chapter Thirteen

Erdun's party was the following night, and he was thrilled with the gift of the aaruul. Tenzin presented him with the box of dry-milk candies in a silk box that probably cost far more than the aaruul ever did, but the old man bowed profusely to both of them, whispered something in Tenzin's ear, and immediately broke off one flower petal and stuck it in his mouth to suck on.

"Success," Tenzin said. "Erdun said he'd been missing them for years and didn't think anyone remembered that he liked them."

"You didn't tell him that Tai told us to get it, did you?"

"Of course not," she said. "You lost a shoe for that candy, Benjamin. I'm not giving the credit to Tai."

He put his arm around her and kissed the top of her head. "That's my tiny thief."

Zhang's banquet hall at the palace was full of humans and vampires, most holding presents in beautifully wrapped packaging for the century-old man who had dedicated his life to serving the elders.

To Ben it felt strange, but he couldn't place why. There was a small, rebellious part of him that wondered if Erdun thought over eighty years of servitude was worth more than a fancy birthday party, but Ben suspected that the thought never crossed Erdun's mind.

Zhang sat on a wide wooden throne with a red silk cushion and intricately carved arms decorated with gold and jade. Zhang wasn't wearing formal white but a sky-blue coat and yellow pants. With his hair down, he looked like he was ready to celebrate.

The guest of honor sat next to Zhang, on a lower seat with similarly carved wooden arms. The chair was tall enough to support an elderly man, but Erdun still sat with ramrod-straight posture. His face was sharply triangular with wide brown eyes and a tufted white beard decorating his narrow chin. He was dressed in his finest regalia—a purple-blue del robe trimmed with gold thread and a red sash—and fitted leather boots.

Humans from all the elders' households and numerous vampires were attending the party. Tenzin had explained that the community of humans serving the elders directly was quite small, and most of them had known each other their entire lives.

Zhang's two closest allies, Elder Lu Dongbin and Elder Xe Xiangu, the Immortal Woman, were also in attendance with their households.

"It's a big party for a human," Ben said. "I'm kind of surprised."

"It's not often that a human reached one hundred years of age," Tenzin said. "Not even on the island. Most die in their nineties." Her eyes flickered. "Nima didn't reach one hundred."

Ben knew that Nima had been a huge part of Tenzin's life, but she rarely talked about her. "It was sooner than you were expecting."

"Her life wasn't easy like those who live here." Tenzin's eyes were fixed on Erdun. "She said she was ready."

Tenzin's casual words didn't match the churn of emotion Ben sensed in her blood. Sadness. Anger. An aching loneliness that felt akin to nostalgia.

And guilt.

"You miss Nima." It was all he could think so say.

"She was with me for nearly eighty years." She glanced at him. "Of course I miss her."

"Did you...?" He frowned. "She didn't want to change."

Tenzin looked up, and her eyes were flashing. "I don't want to talk about Nima."

If Ben hadn't sensed it was important, he wouldn't have pressed. "Why not?"

"This is not the time."

Ben nodded at Erdun. "The guest of honor has dozens of visitors to get through before the banquet and even then, you and I both know we're not really eating. Why don't we go for a walk?"

"Do you think I don't understand what you're doing?"

"No. I think you understand perfectly."

She looked at him, then abruptly marched out of the room.

Ben sighed. "Avoidance, thy name is Tenzin."

———

He found her in the woods to the east of the palace, sitting high in a pine tree that overlooked a frozen pond. The air was still, and in the shelter of the dense pines, the snow swallowed even the sound of the ocean.

In the middle of the grey-frosted pond was an island with a pagoda statue made of deep red-brown clay; its interior flickered with a bright gold flame.

"I knew that at some point I would forget the color of her eyes," Tenzin said. "So I made them find a clay that was as close as I could remember."

"She must have been very beautiful."

"She was stunning." Tenzin's voice was barely a whisper. "She was sunlight." She glanced at him, then back to the pagoda. "Like the flame. They're not supposed to let the lantern go out, but it happens sometimes. She would have told me not to be angry. Humans make mistakes."

"Is this where she's buried?"

"She was cremated by Elder He. Her ashes are here."

Ben perched next to her, keeping his distance. "Why here?"

"It was the part of the gardens she loved the most. Nima loved wild places. Wild things. She made friends with the crows in the mountains. Have you noticed them at the house in Tibet?"

"The crows bring you presents," Ben said. "I thought that was your thing."

She shook her head. "It was Nima. She always left shiny things for them. She fed them and left little pieces of foil or coins. Any shiny thing that caught her eye, she'd leave for them by the house with corn."

"So they bring her gifts even though she's gone now."

"Their children remember her. I told them when she passed, but I don't know if they understood. She loved the gardens in the palace, but she loved wild things the best."

That's why she loved you.

Ben nodded. "This was a good place then. She'd be happy here in the forest."

"She didn't want to change." She looked at Ben. "Like someone else I know."

"Ah." Ben nodded slowly.

"And then years later, there came a time when she changed her mind. But it was too late, she said. I told her it didn't matter, but she..." Tenzin shook her head. "She said she didn't want an aged body for eternity." Her voice was bitter. "As if I would care about that."

"You were angry."

"I was very, *very* angry." Tenzin took a deep breath and let it out. "I wasn't as forgiving then. I refused to see her for almost ten years. She came here to work for Zhang because I didn't want to see her."

Ben closed his eyes. "Tenzin, ten years is a long time for a human."

"I told you I wasn't as forgiving then." Tenzin stared at the lantern. "She loved me more than I deserved."

"Tiny—"

"No." She held up a hand. "Don't say I deserved to be

loved, because I didn't deserve her. I was arrogant. I took her feelings for granted. I knew she feared me at times, and I used that to get what I wanted when she disagreed with me." Tenzin looked at him. "I am not a good person, Benjamin."

He put his arm around her anyway. "We all make mistakes and recognize things we should have done differently over time. That's what shows us we're growing."

"Am I though?" She looked at him. "I was angry when she didn't want to change. I was angry every time you said it too."

So you didn't take a chance with me, did you?

Ben's arm dropped and he looked away. He'd been trying not to relate what had led to his own turning to what had happened between Tenzin and Nima, but it was difficult. Nima had been stubborn about her mortal life, and so had Ben.

They'd had very different fates in the end.

"I can't apologize for it, my Benjamin." She stared at him. "Would you have left me with another lantern to stare at for eternity?"

He drew in a deep breath and let it out slowly. "I don't know what I would have done or said or regretted if I'd stayed human, Tenzin." He stared at the flickering lantern that would forever remind him of the swiftness that was human life, so easily snuffed by the wind.

Inevitably the lantern's fuel would run out, the flame would die, and the stone around it would grow cold. "It wasn't just you," he said. "I recognize that. The universe had other plans for me."

"At the end" —Tenzin turned her eyes back to the lantern

— "Nima said she'd been right not to change. That fate would have judged her for clinging to life instead of accepting rebirth."

"I guess that's one way to see it."

"For her it was the only way." She lifted her chin. "I was with her when she died. I washed her and sang her burial song to send her to her ancestors."

Ben stared at his mate, wondering how often she had performed those rituals for the mortals she had lost. Wondering if she would have sung for him had his fate been different or been too angry to give him that kind of care.

"Tenzin—"

"I know you want to know about my past." She turned to look at him. "Modern humans... you want to know everything. You think that by unearthing ugly things, by revealing *truth*—whatever that means—you will rob those ugly things of their power."

"Are you talking about the very few questions I asked you about Temur? Because I have not pushed—"

"When I am here" —she looked around the woods— "the past feels present. Close to the surface, like the water in that pond, licking against the ice." Tenzin's eyes came to rest on the frozen pond and the glowing flame. "Nima was the only human who ever knew the story of my life, and she took it with her when she died. She asked for it—to give me peace, she said—and I gave it to her." She looked at him. "Do you understand?"

He did. And he didn't. "I don't know what you want me to say. If you're telling me—"

"There is a part of you that wants to make me something

I am not. You want me to change. You want me to evolve, just like you want the island to evolve." She shook her head. "Don't ask me to be something I am not, because the person I have become has been carefully built over a very long time."

"And you want to freeze in time like these islands?" Ben shook his head. "Only dead things don't grow, and you're not dead."

"But I am." She smiled. "I died a very, very long time ago."

He swallowed hard. "You're the most alive person I've ever met in my life. And despite everything, I'm more alive when I'm with you."

She put a hand on his cheek. "In my heart, I know there is nothing I wouldn't give you, Benjamin. Nothing I wouldn't steal or rob or kill to fulfill your wish. If you asked me, I would destroy the world."

His heart was in his throat. "I don't want that, Tenzin."

"Don't ask me for my story, Benjamin." Her eyes shone. "Because eventually I would give it to you, and you would carry it for eternity, not into death and darkness as Nima did."

Ben lifted his chin. "I want all of you."

"You have me." She spread her arms. "As no other has. Can you accept that without asking for more? When I tell you that the blood of Temur is part of a story you do not want and would never understand, can you accept that?"

Can you accept me?

It was far more than secrets she was asking to keep. It was the dark shadows of a life that had transformed her in infinite and frightening ways, lives she had taken, sacrifices she had made, and skin she had shed and shed again, only to become the creature—the woman—he could not live without.

Can you accept that?

"Yes." His heart was heavy, but he wrapped his arms around her and held her to his chest. "I can."

Because turning away from her? It wasn't an option he could face.

Chapter Fourteen

The reception for Elder Han's mate was scheduled to begin at midnight, but with Tai's help, Ben and Tenzin snuck away from the palace an hour after dusk to meet with Jeong, the elderly daoshi who ran the grain storage and mill works for Penglai.

She met them at the eastern gate of the monastery, wearing a black robe with a light grey woolen shirt underneath. She was wrinkled, but her posture was erect and her smile lit up her face. Her silver hair was coiled into a neat bun on top of her head, and a black cap perched atop it. She held a bright brass lantern that illuminated the path for human eyes.

"Greetings to you, Mistress Tenzin and Master Benjamin, esteemed children of Elder Zhang." She bowed and rose to meet their eyes. "Tai has informed me that you have an interest in the grain works and how the provisions for the island are apportioned."

"We do, Daoshi Jeong. Thank you for meeting with us."

She showed them into the monastery grounds, and Ben saw a stretch of fields and neatly divided plots, demonstrating that the monastery garden was far more of a farm than a pleasure garden. Though there were trees and plants everywhere, nearly all of them looked to be edible in some way.

They passed a huge field of cabbage on their right bordered by a line of fruit trees that were bare from winter chill. The smell of frost and winter herbs greeted his nose, and he could scent onions somewhere in the distance.

"As you can see, we don't grow grain here, but our vegetable garden fulfills most of the needs of the palace. It helps, of course, that many of our residents don't eat heavy meals." Her eyes twinkled in the lamplight.

"I confess," Tenzin said, "we have different appetites than the devout."

"But the food is still amazing," Ben said. "Even though we don't eat much. The vegetable soup here is the best in the world."

"You're very kind, Master Benjamin."

"Please just call me Benjamin."

"Of course I cannot," Jeong said smoothly. "The stone building in the center of the monastery is the mill, and the storehouses are behind it. The current mill was built around two hundred years ago with millstones brought from the mainland. It has served us well. I believe there are two smaller mills on Set and Jogé, but they are not as large as ours. They are used mostly for local festivals."

Ben and Tenzin followed Jeong through the garden paths, heading for a hulking building that dominated the center of the modest community. Ben could see numerous animal stables next to it, and the shadow of men and women passing each other with small lanterns as they made their way home for the evening.

"Thank you for the sacrifice of your time, Daoshi," Tenzin said. "We know your day usually ends at dusk."

"Our day is short this time of year," Jeong said. "And the night is long. To accomplish our work, some nighttime activity is necessary. I am at your service, Mistress Tenzin."

"The mills are run by horses?" Ben heard them neighing from the stables.

"Mules," Jeong said. "They are the hardest working. There are many horses on the island, but they are mostly used for riding or horse carts."

Ben remembered the carpenter and the broken harness. Since there were no cars on the islands, people only moved around on foot, by boat, or by horse.

"The horses and mules contribute to the garden," Tenzin said.

"Oh yes." Jeong smiled. "It's all connected. The hay comes from the outer islands when they send the grain. The mules mill the grain, which we send back to the islands that grow it."

"Why not build mills on the islands that grow the grain?" Ben asked.

"The elders must apportion the supplies to each island," Jeong said. "Since every island might produce different crops each year, balancing the supply becomes important."

"And there are islands that don't grow grain at all, right?" Ben asked. "The fishing islands."

She nodded. "You understand."

Jeong pulled the heavy wooden door open and ushered Ben and Tenzin into the stone building. It was freezing with all the workers gone, but he could see large potbellied heaters throughout the building that would warm the mill during the day.

"The grain is bagged on the islands and sent here to the central storehouse. There are five large millstones with five teams that grind the grain throughout the winter season." She pointed to burlap sacks in a corner. "We bag it and take it to the storage house. From there it is counted and sent back to the islands as they have need."

They followed her from the massive mill room through a low door they ducked under, which led into another large chamber where the scent of flour, barley, and corn mixed with dust and the scent of straw.

"As you can see, we have many reserves," Jeong said. "We must ensure that we have enough food for the winter since the vegetables are fewer during the cold season."

Ben noticed several stacks of grain that looked like they were set on top of modern shipping pallets. They took up an entire corner of the storehouse and appeared to be covered in plastic and covered over with wax cloth tarps.

Ben frowned and asked Jeong, "What are those?" He walked over and drew up a corner of the tarp, noting that the writing on the plastic-wrapped bags was in English. There were three densely stacked pallets of grain, all packaged slightly differently.

Jeong's face went carefully blank. "Those are supplemental shipments we have received from Master Myung. I believe he was concerned that our local grain would not be enough for the winter." She smiled. "It was a thoughtful procurement."

So Myung ordered grain the islands didn't need even though—to Ben's eyes—the storehouse looked more than full.

Tenzin was also staring at the shipment from Myung. "Is it milled?"

Ben wondered why she asked.

"Yes, Mistress Tenzin. It is milled and treated. This is not wheat for growing, just for eating."

Tenzin nodded but said nothing else.

"Thank you, Daoshi." Ben walked over and nodded at Jeong. "This has been so interesting. Can I ask you where most of the men and women in the order come from?"

"Those who serve in the palace and the monastery?" Jeong asked.

"Yes. Do they come from the mainland? Or do they—?"

"Rarely from the mainland," Jeong said. "We do have some visiting scholars from libraries and monasteries sponsored by some of the elders like Elder Lu and Elder Han, but they do not work in the fields or the mill. Many of Elder Cao's immortal children come to work here along with Elder Li's."

It made sense that the two earth vampires on the council would have their children working in the gardens.

"But the majority of our brothers and sisters were born right here on the islands. Most families with more than two children will offer one to be raised here at the monastery. The girls with my sisters and me, and the boys with my brothers."

"When did you join the monastery?" he asked.

"I remember no other home than here," Jeong said with a peaceful smile. "I have met my mother and father, but my fellow daoshi are my true family."

———

"HER PARENTS GAVE HER TO THE NUNS," HE MUTTERED under his breath. "She didn't choose it."

Tenzin looked annoyed. "Did she look unhappy?"

"That's not the point."

"Isn't it?"

They were both dressed in their most formal clothing as they stood in the great hall, and both were speaking Spanish instead of Mandarin. Ben knew his sentiments about the monastery and his growing concern with the running of the islands would not be well-received by his mate or the other vampires in the court.

"There are families all over Tibet that also give their sons to the monasteries," Tenzin said. "Should they not be allowed? Often these are poor people who struggle to feed an additional child. At the monasteries—"

"Not the same thing at all," he said quietly. "I've been told over and over again that all the humans on the islands are well provided for. They have plenty to eat and there is no crime. There are jobs for everyone and no one is left out. So why are families offering up a child to the elders like tribute when they get more than two?"

"If the children don't want to live in the monastery when they grow up, no one would force them to stay."

"Would they even know they had options, Tenzin?" He

heard the beat of footsteps on the cobblestones outside. "If that's the only thing you had ever known, would you leave? These are not people who were raised with a plethora of choices in life. This entire system is..."

He didn't say it, but Tenzin raised her eyebrows. She could read what he was thinking and feeling nearly as quickly as he could.

She turned to face the back of the hall as the gates swung open.

Guarded by saffron-clad monks with gold-trimmed caps and richly adorned robes, the doors to the Hall of the Eight Immortals parted, and the vampires in the room turned as one to see the visiting immortals of the South Pacific arrive in full regalia.

Two lines of a dozen warriors with elaborately tattooed skin led the diplomatic party. They were human and pantomimed fearsome faces at the assembled crowd, beating their thighs and chests, chanting a call-and response with their leader. Ben and Tenzin had been informed that while the presentation might appear aggressive, this was a traditional greeting from Sina's court and was intended to honor and respect the host, not intimidate or frighten.

The halls of Penglai were transfixed as a dozen women came behind them, half of them holding traditional spears, blades, and shields and the other half bearing massive baskets of colorful flowers. Their legs were tattooed with geometric patterns, and all of them had masses of dark hair that fell to their waist or longer.

The vampires came next, two immortal warriors with similar appearance to the human warriors, guarding a tall woman Ben guessed had to be Mahina judging from the sudden brightness that came to the normally dour face of Elder Han.

He could immediately tell why Jae had been so impressed with her. She was nearly as tall as Ben, with dark eyes rimmed with thick lashes, full red lips, and tumbled curls that fell past her waist.

"I don't think I've ever seen one of our kind who looked more living," Tenzin said. "She's a stunning vampire."

Mahina wore a traditional wrapped dress in shades of orange and brown that set off her skin, which was glowing and still appeared sun-kissed, though she was thousands of years old.

Behind Mahina were two more vampire guards who walked on either side of a small woman, and whatever Ben had imagined Sina's appearance might be, it was not what he saw.

Sina, ancient of the Pacific Sea, looked hardly older than Tenzin. Her deep brown skin was free of any tattoos, but her eyes were highlighted by intricate white and yellow face paint. Her hair was a tightly curled light blond, twisted into thin locs that coiled on top of her head like a crown. Sina wore a dress of deep red and a massive necklace made of gold and colorful shells.

Power radiated off the small vampire, and she made no attempt to hide it. As she walked down the center of the hall, Ben could see her effect on the immortals nearest her amnis. There was more than one quiet gasp, and whispers buzzed around the room.

Ben glanced at Tenzin, who was watching Sina with wide eyes.

"What is it?"

Tenzin couldn't seem to take her eyes off the woman. "I want to know her."

"Why? Even from here, I feel like she could suck us dry and leave us a husk of our former selves."

"I know." Tenzin's eyes were bright. "Don't you want to know her?"

He shook his head. "You're a very strange woman."

Mahina and Sina reached the front of the hall, and every elder on the dais rose and—as if via a secret signal—bowed at a precise forty-five-degree angle. The bows were returned by Mahina, Sina, and their entourage.

Elder Han was the one who spoke to the assembly. "Most honored Sina of the south, mother of oceans and Rumak of the Fire Islands," he said. "And my dear and honored mate, Mahina, daughter of the dragon king and holder of the Heilala Throne, you and your company are most welcome in the court of Penglai. It has been too long since your people have favored us with a visit such as this."

Sina nodded but didn't say anything. Mahina motioned to the humans with them, who placed elaborately decorated weapons, large rolls of red and orange cloth, and mounds of flowers at the base of the dais.

"Elder Han," Mahina said. "My sire and I are most grateful for the welcome of the Elders of Penglai, and we request a private audience with you and Elder Lu Dongbin when it is favorable to you."

Though there had been a temporary seal put in place,

there was no doubt in Ben's mind they wanted to know what had happened to Mahina's Eye.

"We may be getting a call," he whispered to Tenzin.

"I expect so." She kept her eyes on the dais, where Elder Han was responding to his mate.

"Of course." He stepped off the dais. "Your journey has been long." Elder Han was clearly ready to have his mate to himself. "Allow us to see to your comfort here in the palace."

The vampires from the south departed with their entourage, and the formal gathering in the great hall started to break apart. Ben's thoughts were bouncing around as vampires and humans milled about.

What would Sina say about the disappearance of the Pearl Seal?

What would they say to Sina?

Would Elder Han and Mahina be able to announce her move during the visit as they had intended?

Ben and Tenzin still had no idea where the seal might have gone, and he could hardly justify his wild hair about grain supplies on the island being pertinent to the investigation they had been tasked to head.

Did Tenzin really want to get to know the tiny, frightening water vampire who was even older than she was?

But really, why the hell had Myung ordered extra grain from the mainland, and could it have anything to do with the theft of the seal?

"It's a delicate balance."

He turned and saw Tenzin watching him. "What?"

"All this. The *system* you were talking about. The humans on the island. The monastery. The vampire courts.

The rituals. The presentation of gifts and the delicate scales of favors, alliances, and territory." She stepped closer and switched to Spanish again. "I knew our world before this, Benjamin, when negotiation was done at the edge of a blade." She looked around. "All this—the court, the island, the priests, the people who make all of it happen? I may chafe at the formality, but those careful systems have maintained peace for thousands of years. It's diplomacy instead of conquest."

"I'm not denying that," Ben said. "But does that mean it's as good as it can be? That it can't get better?" He looked around. "Not just for the vampires. For everyone?"

She stared at him, and her eyes didn't waver. "If you want to make something new, my Benjamin, be aware of what you unmake in the process."

Chapter Fifteen

A s Tenzin had expected, they were called to Elder Han's compound less than an hour after Sina and Mahina had arrived. When they walked into the entry hall-way, Jae met them with a nervous expression on his face.

"Sina is very unhappy." He was all but wringing his hands. "Mahina's Eye was rare and huge. She dove for the pearl herself, and seeing it gone..."

"Calm yourself," Tenzin said with authority. "We're going to find it, but careful investigation takes time. I'll make sure she understands."

Tenzin was trying hard not to let her excitement at meeting Sina show in her expression. Though she could feel Ben's skepticism through their mating bond, she felt nothing but anticipation at meeting the mysterious ancient that so few had ever seen.

Jae led them into a meeting room that had been deco-rated with lush tropical plantings. The room was heated nearly to uncomfortable levels, and the windows were dripping with condensation from the cold air outside.

Inside the reception room, the air smelled of earth, lush greenery, and tropical blooms. Heat emanated from the floor, and the humidity in the room dampened her amnis.

Clever, clever Sina.

Her eyes met the ancient's and locked. Sina watched Tenzin with as much interest as Tenzin watched Sina.

"Daughter of Zhang." Sina didn't wait for their introduction. "Long have I heard stories of your prowess in battle. Better still for us to meet here in peace."

"Sina of the Fire Islands." Tenzin bowed deeply. "It is my honor to meet one of such renown."

"I try to keep my renown in check." Her dark eyes were amused. "I have found the less the world knows of me, the better it is for my survival."

Was it Tenzin's imagination, or was the water in the air reaching for her exposed skin? She felt it in the space around her, trying to dampen her elemental power. In reaction, the air in the room hugged her and Ben, unsure of this foreign presence, clinging to them as they waited for Sina's water to settle down.

The silent elemental battle made the leaves of the tropical greenery around them rustle as the air and the water bounced and deflected in the room. The dripping on the windows was audible as water dropped and pooled on the wooden floor, misted again from the heat, and dissolved into the room.

"Mother." Mahina's voice cut through the tension.

"Enough. Elder Zhang's children are here to help find the pearl."

"Ah." Sina's eyes never wavered from Tenzin. "Is that so?"

"Yes." Tenzin's amnis reached out for Benjamin, and when it touched his power, she felt her amnis grow stronger, more confident, and press against the water with more vigor. "We have experience in finding objects that have been lost or stolen."

"And this object?" Sina asked. "Was it lost? Or was it stolen?"

Ben spoke for the first time. "Perhaps it was stolen by the lost."

Sina broke her gaze with Tenzin and turned her eyes to Ben. "An interesting perspective, Benjamin Vecchio, son of Zhang and guardian of Mithra's scroll."

So Sina knew about the Bone Scroll. Excellent. Though Ben was still learning Ge'ez and his uncle was still trying to decipher the language of the scroll so they could read it, simply having access to it was enough to make other vampires respect his presence.

"It's an honor to meet you," Ben said. "Elder Han and those of his household speak so highly of your daughter Mahina." He turned on his charm and directed it toward Elder Han's mate. "It's a pleasure to finally meet you. We've been anticipating your arrival for days now."

"But you still haven't found the Pearl Seal?" Mahina asked. "I understand one of Cheng's people was here and had opportunity."

"We visited Cheng personally and determined that while

139

his business interests are... varied, it doesn't make sense for him to have taken the Pearl Seal, nor would he be likely to do so. His ambition is without question, but so is his respect for you, your mother, and the sanctity of Penglai."

Wow. If Ben thought Tenzin wasn't going to tell Cheng that he'd just sung the pirate's praises in public, he was dead wrong. She was impressed by her mate's confidence. She could feel his trepidation though his blood and amnis, but not a drop of it showed on his face or in his voice.

"Careful investigation takes time." Tenzin nodded to Mahina. "We *will* find the Pearl Seal, Mistress Mahina. And we will find the one who stole it."

"Very well." Mahina turned from them and faced Elder Han. "Sina and I would like to feed now. Our journey was long, and the seas were rough."

Tenzin bowed; Ben followed. And she kept her eyes on Sina's as she backed out of the room.

Another time, the ancient's expression said.

Another time.

———

"WHAT THE HELL WAS THAT?" BEN LET OUT A LONG breath when they reached the open air. "Come on." He took to the sky and shook the last of the water from his skin. Tenzin followed as he flew upward and out of the palace, coming to rest in the snow-tipped bamboo forest that bordered the southeastern side of the island and overlooked the Pearl Gate.

Ben sat on a stone wall that had a view of the dock, and

the bamboo rustled in the frosty air behind him.

"She reminds me of Kato." Ben could only compare Sina to the other water ancient that he knew. "But not as nice."

"Kato is your uncle's grandsire." Tenzin came to sit next to him. "He likes you, so of course you think he's nice. Sina doesn't know us."

"But you'd like to know her?"

Tenzin shrugged. "Of course. She's powerful. Who knows, maybe she is older than Saba."

"No." Ben shook his head. "She doesn't feel as old."

"You're just saying that because you know Saba better."

"No, I'm saying that because everything about Sina feels... hotter somehow. Newer."

"She is of the water, but also the fire," Tenzin said. "All her islands were formed in fire. The fire lives under the ocean in her territory. To her, fire is as familiar as blood."

"I hadn't thought about that." Ben frowned. "We need to focus on the seal. We've been chasing this weird thing with Myung and the grain, but that doesn't really have anything to do with what we were hired to do."

"Technically we weren't hired." Tenzin pouted. "They're not going to pay us."

"We'll be paid in a favor owed."

"They already owe me dozens of favors," Tenzin muttered. "But fine. Yes, they will surely grant us a favor, and I am thinking of asking for the favor of inspecting the treasury."

"What treasury?" Ben frowned. "There's a treasury?"

The corner of her mouth turned up. "Of course there's a

treasury. Do you think all the gifts that are brought to them simply disappear?"

Ben hadn't thought about it, but every single time a formal delegation arrived, they always came bearing gifts. Of course the elders would have a treasury to store them all. "Well, where's the treasury?"

"Beneath the palace," Tenzin said. "Elder Cao's people guard it."

"The same Elder Cao who has his children working at the monastery?"

"Yes, but I don't think that has anything to do with anything," Tenzin said. "Why do you have a sudden interest in the treasury?"

He looked at her. "Seriously? Because an artifact was taken, and we're assuming it was the first one."

Tenzin's eyebrows went up. "You think someone is stealing from the treasury?"

"I think it's possible, don't you? Has anyone checked?"

"I have no idea. Who would steal from the elders' treasury? There are guards whose only job is to watch over the doors."

"And during the day?"

"It's underground and it's locked."

Ben shook his head. "The blind spots. The blind spots are what still get me." He stood and brushed off his robes. "Come on."

"What are we doing?"

"We're going to check with Elder Cao and see if anyone has an inventory that we can check. At some point you and Jae and everyone else are going to have to admit that some mysterious felon didn't land on the island and make off with the seal. This was an inside job, and I have a feeling that the Pearl Seal might not be the only thing that's gone missing from this place."

They flew back to the palace garden, but as soon as they landed, Gan, Zhang's chief of guard, ambushed them with a snap and a severe expression that said *Don't ask questions.*

Ben and Tenzin exchanged a look, then followed her into Zhang's entry hall. The vampire turned to them, her face in torment.

"You need to get to Penglai town right now." She swallowed hard. "A human has been murdered."

————

Tianyu ran into his house, shut the door, and leaned against the solid wood surface, his heart still racing.

Had anyone seen him?

Did they know?

It was all turning sour. The careful plan was falling apart, and if the vampires from the palace found him and discovered what he'd done, Tianyu would be dead. There were no such things as trials on Penglai. The elders would judge him guilty, and that would be that. Jiayi would be an orphan, lingering in the shadows of Penglai town for the rest of her life, forgotten and shamed, then die in anonymity like her parents.

He took the bundle he'd shoved in his coat and hid it under the bed where the cursed Pearl Seal was still wrapped and hidden.

What should he do? There was no one who could help him, no one who would understand that all of it was spinning out of control like a horse cart with a broken harness running wild on a downhill road.

Horse carts.

Harnesses.

The sight of Haitao's broken and bloodied body would haunt Tianyu for the rest of his life. He'd only gone to the harness maker's house to pay the man off. All he had wanted was silence.

How had all this gone so horribly, horribly wrong?

Forgive me, Shuang! Have mercy on your poor, foolish husband. I was trying to do the right thing.

All I wanted...

It didn't matter what he had wanted. Part of him wanted to take the Pearl Seal and fling the cursed dragon into the sea. Maybe then no one would ever know of his crimes. Maybe there was a way he could sneak onto the mainland. Surely the papers people spoke of in hushed whispers weren't that important.

They were only papers after all. How important could papers be?

There had to be those who would hire a skilled carpenter on the mainland, someone who worked well with horses and could fix a wheel before you could finish a cup of tea. Surely he could manage in the outside world.

He had to get off Penglai Island. Maybe if he took a trip out to the outer islands, he could find a boat that would take him and Jiayi to the mainland without the magistrate knowing. Was there a good excuse for Tianyu and his small daughter to visit one of the outer islands? Maybe there was a shrine that had been dear to Shuang, who had been born on Set?

Someone pounded on the front door.

"Tianyu!" A deep voice shouted his name. "Come to the door! Quickly! Something terrible has happened!"

You don't know. You don't understand. So many terrible things have happened that I have lost count.

Tianyu wiped the panic sweat from his forehead and tried to compose his face. Then he tore his outer coat off, unbound his hair, and wrapped his housecoat around himself as if he were just rising from bed. He walked to the door and cracked it open.

"What's wrong?"

Chapter Sixteen

B en and Tenzin surveyed the scene in silence. Three vampire guards from the palace stood in the narrow street outside, and another was positioned in the alley behind the house.

The small cottage was behind a leather shop where harnesses, aprons, and tools hung in the windows. Inside the attached living area, saddles sat on wooden frames around the room, blocking two of the doors. The windows were wide open, the cold wind whipped through the house, and the smell of woodsmoke permeated the air from a bellowing stove in the corner.

"I can't smell anything but smoke, ice, and mud," Tenzin said. "Whoever did this knew vampires would come."

And they didn't want to leave a scent behind.

Ben was tempted to close the windows, but he didn't want to move anything until he'd formed a mental picture of the small wooden house where a lifeless body lay on the floor.

The human was bloody and bruised with numerous cuts

on his face and hands. He'd been struck from behind by a long, thin hammer with a narrow square head on one side and a thin, piercing point on the other, which was still embedded in his skull.

Ben crouched down and spoke in a low voice, keeping his words in Spanish to avoid immortal ears outside. "Tiny, this is not our thing." He looked up. "We find valuables, not murderers."

Tenzin echoed his quiet voice. "You don't think this has to do with the Pearl Seal?"

He rose. "We have no idea. We can't even find the thief because no one seems willing to admit that it was probably an inside job."

Tenzin pointed at the body. "Perhaps he had something to do with it."

Ben had doubts that a seemingly crude harness and saddle maker would be behind the theft of a gold-and-jade seal, but there was something tickling the back of his memory, and he couldn't settle on it. There were too many thoughts flying around his mind, too many senses on alert.

The sickly-sweet scent of the man's cold blood, the sweat ingrained within his blankets and clothes, the woodsmoke and a hint of stale bread. The smell of sweat and stale bread triggered a memory of his childhood, and he was back in an alley when he was seven years old, staring at the broken body of a man in a red hoodie behind the bakery.

"Ben?"

He blinked and remembered where he was. "We don't do this, Tenzin. Maybe we should call—"

"We have to do this." Her voice was barely audible. "If

we do not, the town authorities will find someone to blame in order to pacify the elders, execute that person, and move on. They will not care if it's truly the murderer or not."

Ben ignored the spike of anger in his blood and nodded. "Fine. You're right."

She nodded and continued in a normal voice, conscious of the guards outside. "It looks like he was beaten first. Then the hammer blow came at the end."

Ben crouched down and looked at the man's frozen face. "Yeah, he was in bad shape even before he was killed. Could have been a human or a vampire."

"Vampires don't kill like this." Tenzin shook her head.

"They might if they didn't want anyone to know a vampire did it." Ben stood and looked around the room. "We all have fists, Tiny." He nodded at the potbellied stove in the corner. "He lived alone, and the fire was built up. Could he have been expecting company?"

"It's a cold night," Tenzin said. "He could have wanted to read a book or do some work by the fire."

"He lived alone?"

"Neighbors say his parents lived with him until their death, but he never married. He learned the leather trade from his father."

Ben looked around the room at the low, worn couches, the stacks of bowls and mugs in the small kitchen area, and the closed door that led to a cold bedroom. "It looks like he slept in here in the winter. One room is easier to keep warm."

"Agreed." Tenzin reached for the hammer. "Should I?"

Ben nodded. "I guess so. I mean, it's not like they're going to call the crime lab, right?"

"There's never been a murder like this on the island." Tenzin removed the hammer from the man's skull and lifted it to her nose to smell the handle. "Leather."

"In a saddle shop." Ben huffed out a breath. "Imagine that."

"Or the killer wore leather gloves."

"Again, could be either a human or a vampire who wants us to think it was a human. What do you mean 'a murder like this'?"

"What?" She looked at him with a frown.

"You said there'd never been a murder *like this* on Penglai."

"Oh." Tenzin waved a hand. "Over the centuries there have been drunken idiots who fought and one accidentally killed the other. There have been husbands or wives who killed their spouse in a rage. But nothing like this. Someone plotted to kill this man."

"Or it could have been a fight gone wrong."

"The hammer came from the shop in front." She looked at the side door that led to the harness workshop. "Someone brought it here with the intent to kill this human."

"I don't know, Tiny. It looks like he worked in the evenings, so it's possible the victim might have brought the hammer from the shop and it was just lying around."

"And the killer grabbed it and killed him with it during an argument?"

Ben shrugged. "We should find out who had business with him. Maybe they argued over a bill."

Tenzin raised an eyebrow. "You don't really think this has anything to do with an angry customer, do you?"

"No." Ben walked to the side and leaned against a door-post when he felt a new vampire approaching the house. "I don't."

The unknown vampire stayed outside the door with the guards, and a group of four humans came into the small house with a canvas stretcher that looked like it was out of a historic movie.

One of the men addressed them in a low voice. "The magistrate has sent us to take Haitao's body to the temple so it can be prepared for burial."

The magistrate? Ben looked at Tenzin, and she mouthed, *Myung*.

She asked, "Does he have any family?"

The human said, "He has cousins on his father's side, and the daoshi have already been called."

Ben watched the four humans. Two of them couldn't seem to look at the body. Queasy stomachs or guilty minds?

Tenzin came to stand next to him as the four men lifted the dead body, which had started to become stiff. The humans who hadn't been able to look at the body both appeared pale, but Ben still couldn't tell if they were squeamish or ashamed.

"Stop," Tenzin said. "Put him down."

Ben half expected Tenzin to look at something on the body, but she must have noticed the two men's reluctance too, because as soon as they set the body down, she was in the face of the first pale human.

"Did you kill him?"

The man's eyes widened; then he shook his head. "No." He held out his hand. "You may ask me again if you wish."

Ask me with amnis. It was as good a proof of innocence as anything.

She turned to the second man. "And you?"

The man's shoulders were slumped, his eyes full of sorrow. "I didn't hurt him, but... I owed him money. I promise I will pay his family."

Tenzin narrowed her eyes, then nodded silently. "Your name?"

"Hwan, the tailor."

She turned to the other man. "And you?"

"Lim. I tend the gardens in the town."

The first human spoke again, and an edge of irritation colored his voice. "And I am Jinhai. This is my brother Shen. As I said, Myung sent us, and we should take him to the temple." He bowed deeply, possibly regretting his words. "That is unless you have any other questions."

Tenzin looked at the man. "Not right now; you may go."

Jinhai bowed again. "Thank you, Lǎoshī."

They once again lifted the stretcher and, with some difficulty, maneuvered the body out of the small room. Left behind was a black pool of sticky blood that was congealing on the wooden floor of the house.

Tenzin bent down, stuck her finger in it, and licked it.

"Tenzin!" Ben curled his lip. "What if he was poisoned or something?"

She shrugged. "It's not like it would hurt me. I think he's been dead for about four hours."

Ben looked at the old-fashioned clock on the wall. "So before Sina's arrival."

"It was a busy time at the palace; a vampire could have

snuck away without it being noticed." Tenzin stood and walked toward Ben. "A human could have visited him with even less notice. There are no streetlights here, and most go to sleep not long after the sun goes down."

"So we can ask neighbors," he said, "but it's likely no one would notice if the harness maker had a visitor."

The amnis that had been lingering outside entered the room, and Myung nodded at both of them. "The humans will care for the body, but I doubt you'll find any who will have seen Haitao's killer. As Tenzin said, most humans are home after dark. This house isn't near the tavern or the meeting hall, so most of his neighbors were probably already sleeping."

Ben had thoughts, but Tenzin pushed a negative energy through their mating bond and he remained silent.

"What did you know of the harness maker?" Tenzin asked.

"Not more than I know of any craftsman here in the town. He was a hard worker. I never had a complaint against him for cheating, shoddy work, or the usual petty problems the humans have when they bicker with each other."

There was a thread of disdain in Myung's voice that was hard to miss.

"You are their magistrate," Ben said, "so you hear their petitions if there are disagreements."

Myung turned his eyes to Ben. "I do."

"But nothing against Haitao?" Tenzin asked. "What could be the motive for someone to kill him?"

"Perhaps he was sleeping with another man's wife or something of that nature."

Tenzin raised her eyebrows and looked around the room that was clearly meant for a bachelor and not for company. Dirty dishes in the kitchen, piles of work, and empty jugs of beer accompanied the thick scent of sweat and woodsmoke from a poorly ventilated room.

"Yes," she said. "I can see how that would be possible."

Ben bit his lip to keep from smiling. "We'll continue looking for who killed the man." He cleared his throat. "Thank you for your insight, Myung."

Ben's eyes moved from Myung to the door, then back to Myung. He kept staring silently until the other vampire turned to Tenzin.

"I will leave you to your work," Myung said. "Please let me or Elder Lu know if you need anything else."

He left the small house, and Ben felt his amnis drifting away as the vampire put more distance between them.

"Did you notice how he inserted his sire's name in there at the end?" Ben kept his voice quiet and switched from Mandarin to Spanish again.

"I did." Tenzin crouched down to examine the bloodstain again, then looked at the door. "Everyone on Penglai Island has secrets, but I'm beginning to think Myung has more than the rest."

———

COLD RAIN BATTERED THE TILE ROOF OVER BEN AND Tenzin's heads as the winter dawn approached and vampires, humans, and animals took shelter from the freezing cold front passing over the islands.

"We need to head back to the States soon," Ben said. "I promised my sister I'd be in Los Angeles for Christmas."

"We will finish this. Then we will go to Christmas." Tenzin was wrapped around Ben under a heavy silk quilt. Neither of them produced body heat without conscious thought, so when Ben slept during the day, she kept him warm.

He didn't need to be warm, but it was an aspect of his humanity that Tenzin found she missed. Whether Ben missed it or not was debatable, but either way, she liked to keep them warm.

"We'll go to Los Angeles and buy presents," he said. "And look at the palm trees wrapped in pretty lights. And maybe cruise around the marina and look at the boats."

"I like presents."

Ben kissed the top of her head. "Your skin feels like the surface of the sun, Tenzin."

"It's cold outside."

He chuckled a little. "And this affects us how?"

"Be quiet and sleep."

His arms hugged her tighter. "I've been thinking about what you said earlier."

"At the monastery, Mahina's reception, in the forest, or at the murder scene?"

Ben was silent for a long moment. "This was a fucking busy night."

"I am still processing most of it." Tenzin looked up and met his eyes. "What did I say earlier?"

"That you remember life before all this. That diplomacy is better than conquest and I need to remember what I might unmake in the process of trying to make something better."

"Hmm." She'd almost forgotten about that. She'd said it more to assuage Ben's feelings than to guide him. He was powerful, but he wasn't as powerful as the Eight. And if the elders wanted to keep island society the same as it had been for thousands of years?

Ben wasn't going to change that.

"I'm not talking about remaking the islands. I really do think that the majority of the people here are happy and content. You're right; they're not complaining."

"I do love it when you say I'm right."

"Ha ha." He pinched the delicate skin where her thigh met her buttock. "I know what you're saying, but I still think I'm right too."

"How so?"

"Choices." He tipped her chin up to look at him. "Think of it this way: the humans on the island are people, but the elders see them as resources, don't they?"

"That may sound cold, but you are correct."

"Many of those people are fisherman and farmers and seamstresses and artisans who make this place run. They're happy and successful. In fact, in the outside world, the skills many of them have wouldn't be nearly as important as they are here."

She nodded. "You're correct again."

"But there are others who *are* unhappy. I guarantee it. And what if there are some of those people—those resources —who might be exceptional businesspeople or computer scientists or doctors, working in immortal organizations on the mainland? If you think of it that way, those are resources that aren't being used well or wisely."

Her eyebrows rose. "This is an argument that could be persuasive."

"I thought so."

She turned her head and kissed him. "You're really quite clever. I'm very impressed with myself that I chose you as a mate."

Ben smiled. "That was the weirdest self-centered compliment I've ever received. Thanks."

"You're welcome."

Chapter Seventeen

The following night, Ben and Jae planned to return to Penglai town and the murder scene while Tenzin and her father discreetly inspected the treasury. Ben didn't notice how cold the night was until he arrived at the front gate to see Jae wearing an extra layer beneath a heavy canvas jacket.

"It's cold." Ben saw Jae's breath steaming in the air. "We can take a carriage if you wish."

"No, the walk will warm me up." Jae turned and headed out the gate, walking under a brilliant gold dragon seal surrounded by carved jade and intricate wooden fretwork.

Ben looked up at the golden seal. "Was the Pearl Seal like this?"

Jae glanced at the Dragon Gate. "A little. A dragon, but not as elaborate as this one. Older design, and with the pearl for the eye instead of a ruby."

Ben blinked when he realized that was the large stone that glinted black in the darkness. "And it's just *here*. Out in the open. No alarms. No guards. Nothing."

"Other than the palace guards, no." Jae raised an eyebrow. "Before the Pearl Seal was taken, I would have asked you, 'Who would steal from the Eight Immortals?' But obviously someone would." He turned and started down the cobblestone road while Ben had to constrain the urge to take to the sky and jump down the hill toward the village to speed things up.

"I'm getting as impatient as Tenzin these days," he muttered.

Jae turned and smiled, clearly understanding Ben's frustration. "You may fly ahead if you wish. I will walk quickly to catch up."

"No, this is good for me." He took a deep, needless breath. "Sometimes I think I've forgotten too quickly what it means to be human."

"Do you miss it?" Jae quickly added, "Sorry, that's none of my business."

"It's fine." Ben cocked his head. "I miss things about being human, but I was living with vampires for so long before my change it was a... natural transition. Other than missing the sun, my life isn't that much different."

Except for mating with Tenzin. That was definitely different.

And craving the taste of blood.

And smelling everything on earth, the good and the bad. Ben was still getting accustomed to that not-usually-pleasant surprise. Life could really stink. Literally stink.

So maybe it wasn't as smooth as he'd expressed, but in the past year, Ben had felt as if he was settling into immortal life and getting over the shock of his transition.

He didn't always turn in shock at the stranger in the mirror with the inhuman eyes. He'd grown to love the caress of the wind through his hair and the utter adoration and rightness he felt when he was at one with his element. Then there was the passage of time.

The winter holidays had arrived with such speed this year it was as if six months had passed in the blink of an eye. He was learning to plan—not in months but in years.

"I've become more and less patient at the same time," Ben said to Jae. "If Tenzin and I are planning a job, I find myself thinking it could be this year or next, but as long as it gets done, that's all that's important. And yet the slowness of walking does begin to irritate me." He smiled. "But not when I have company."

Jae nodded. "I have never had a desire for immortality. I find myself content with the idea of growing older. I'd like to marry and have a family if the elders bless me to do so." He smiled. "That said, I do see the appeal of flying."

"I can't lie. Flying is very cool. Except for the bugs."

Jae frowned. "I've never thought about the bugs."

"It's one of the reasons we wear black."

They reached the outskirts of Penglai town and saw the extra palace guards strolling through the city, roughly half human and half vampire.

The mood was hushed as Ben and Jae walked through the town, and Ben could see the usual peace and joviality of Penglai had been bruised by the death of the harness maker.

"It's a shock to them," Jae said. "Murders don't happen here. Fights sometimes. And I remember once, when my father was young, two brothers got into a horrible fistfight and one accidentally killed the other. It was a tragedy that people spoke of for decades."

"But other than that?"

Jae looked around the town and nodded at the passing humans. "Violence of any kind is a sign that something is out of balance, and Penglai prides itself on balance. Everyone has their role on the islands. Everyone has a place to live, food to eat, and a job to do. Why would violence appear here?"

They arrived at Haitao's house where two human guards wearing Myung's deep blue uniform were standing. They nodded to Jae and bowed to Ben as they stepped aside to clear the door.

Ben and Jae entered the house, and Jae looked around with a deep sigh.

"I don't remember this man, but any violent death is terrible."

Ben wondered how the humans on the island that seemed to love peace and nonviolence so much reconciled that fact with the immutable truth that they worshipped and served creatures that were capable perpetrators of brutal and efficient violence.

Because if there was one thing Ben knew without a doubt, a vampire did not attain the status of a god among immortals without being willing to do what it took to maintain their power. Sure, they'd taken vows of nonviolence on Penglai and dedicated themselves to peace, but that was now.

Everyone had a history.

Jae pointed to the saddles and the harnesses lying around the house. "Clearly Haitao was a hard worker, and he played an important role in the village."

"The men who came to get him seemed to be friendly, but they said he didn't have a family."

"It's not unusual." Jae started poking around the house. "People on the outer islands have larger families. The craftsmen and artisans here on Penglai might have one or two children, but more than one is considered an indulgence. Many don't marry at all but focus only on their work."

"Interesting." In theory, someone without any living family didn't have bonds that could be used against them. They could be more reckless. Would a single and childless harness maker have risked the wrath of the elders to steal the Pearl Seal? Maybe he wanted a new life? Maybe he was just greedy.

Ben poked his head outside and asked one of Myung's men, "Where did this man spend his time? Did he have friends?"

Both the men looked confused. "We didn't know him, master."

"Who would?"

"Perhaps you could ask at the tavern," the other man said. "I smelled beer inside. Maybe he didn't always like to drink alone."

"Good thinking."

The man looked pleased. "Thank you."

Ben went back inside to see Jae crouched on the ground, looking at the pool of blood.

"Ben, come look at this." He pointed at something just barely touching a drop of blood on the edge of the stain. "Do you see it?"

Ben bent down. "It's a tiny piece of wood."

"It's a *curl* of wood." Jae picked it up delicately between two fingers. "Like it was chiseled or possibly came from a manual drill."

"Okay." Ben looked around the room, up at the ceiling, then back at the curl of wood. "I don't see any woodworking equipment in this place. So someone brought it here."

"And it was on *top* of the blood." Jae said. "The wood is fresh and lay on top of the blood. That means whoever left it here possibly worked with wood or was around a woodworker and picked it up on their clothes."

"Then they left it here *after* Haitao was dead."

"Yes. According to Elder Han's head of guard, the body was found by a fisherman who was walking down the docks before dawn and saw the door open. He went inside and saw the dead man, then immediately went to the village guard who reported it to Myung."

There was Myung's name again. "The fisherman is not likely to have wood shavings on his clothes is what you're saying."

"Not likely at all." Jae sat back on his heels. "But a carpenter or woodworker is, and they might even have a connection to the Pearl Seal."

Ben smiled. "The men who were working on the renovations."

"Exactly." Jae stood. "Let's go back to Myung's. We need to know the name of the carpenter who worked on that gate."

———

TENZIN HAD KNOWN LOVE IN HER LIFE. SHE remembered her mother's songs when she fell asleep at night. The young man who had been her first husband had loved her. Nima's love had comforted her and coaxed her toward life after thousands of years in darkness.

And Ben's love? His love was the wind at her back and the fire that made her heart beat.

But what she saw before her?

Her sire put a firm hand on her shoulder. "It does not belong to you."

Tears threatened the corners of Tenzin's eyes as she stared at the neatly organized rows of gold artifacts, mountains of jewelry, glass, gems, silk, and porcelain. The treasury of the Eight Immortals was a well of riches while the grandeur of the palace above it was only a faint trickle of water hiding the true depth of ancient wealth.

"But it does belong to you—in part—and I am your heir." Tenzin couldn't tear her eyes away. "You granted me that role two thousand years ago, and you can't take it back. So in a sense—"

"This treasury belongs to the Eight Immortals," Zhang said. "The office and the island, not the elders as individuals."

"Details." She let out a slow breath and eyed a ruby the size of her fist. "Where is that from?"

Zhang looked at the vampire treasurer who held a massive ledger. "Maria?" The woman was a child of Elder Cao's, the earth vampire who had dug this treasury from the rock of the island and whose children were entrusted with its safekeeping.

"The blood ruby of Konark," the treasurer said. "A gift to the Immortal Woman in the early fourteenth century."

I want it.

"Tenzin." Her father's voice was a warning.

She sighed and turned to the treasurer. "Have you noticed anything missing from the treasury?"

Maria frowned. "We keep track of any item in the treasury that is loaned or borrowed for ceremonial purposes. None of them—"

"I'm talking about a thief," Tenzin said. "The Pearl Seal was stolen under the eyes of the elders; I am trying to determine if other items were taken."

Maria blinked. "You suspect a thief has found their way into the treasury?" She narrowed her eyes. "Nothing has been reported to me, but give me a few moments."

The vampire left Tenzin and Elder Zhang waiting near an intricately carved table with velvet trays, glass cases, and paperwork scattered along the top.

Tenzin turned to Zhang. "What is she doing?"

"Maria has a unique gift." Zhang watched the blur of movement that erupted in the rows of gold, glass, and gems. "Elder Cao found her and turned her for this specific purpose."

"What is her gift?"

"Eidetic memory," he said. "Some call it total recall. Maria was working in a clerk's office in Manila when Elder Cao's son met her and discovered what she could do. Elder Cao saw her potential at once."

"So she doesn't just have a ledger," Tenzin said. "She *is* a ledger? She remembers what every shelf in the treasury looks like?"

Zhang nodded. "She's organized it over the past century," he said. "Quite a remarkable feat considering its size. And highly useful. When official visitors are arriving at the palace, the palace staff can always come to Maria to see what artifacts or works of art should be put on display in the gallery. She knows the history of every one."

"Fascinating."

Tenzin and Zhang had no sooner finished chatting about Maria's remarkable accomplishment than the vampire finished her survey of the treasury.

She met them back at the table with fury in her eyes. "There are three items missing, and they have not been logged."

Tenzin said, "And if they're not logged?"

"They're stolen."

Chapter Eighteen

The town hall was a simple structure with a heated wooden floor, whitewashed plaster walls, and a traditional thatch roof. The rain was still beating down when Jae and Ben gathered the group of six men inside. They sat them all at a low table in the center of the room and waited while the men drank the tea palace stewards prepared for them.

All the men had worked on the gate, and all of them had an account with Haitao.

One had ordered a saddle.

Two were waiting for broken harnesses to be mended.

One didn't have any work outstanding, but according to the tavern keeper, he and Haitao had argued about a woman months ago.

Two more were there because they'd worked on the gate and their names were in Haitao's ledger, but Ben didn't think they were strong suspects.

"It's possible that one of them came in and found the

body but was afraid to tell anyone," Jae said. "It's hard to imagine that any of these men are murderers."

"Do you think I look like a killer?" Ben asked.

Jae blinked. "You're an immortal, so of course—"

"The first man I ever killed was when I was human," Ben said. "I was a sixteen-year-old kid. He had a gun and I had a knife. I stabbed him to death."

Jae was silent.

"I was protecting a friend and her baby, but I still killed him, and I did not hesitate to do it," Ben said. "Anyone is capable of murder if the circumstances are right."

Jae nodded. "I understand."

"It might have been an accident. It might have been a crime of passion." He motioned his head toward the men. "We need to find out."

"Of course." Jae walked over to the men and sat down.

The men stopped whispering among each other and looked at Jae; a few of them glanced at Ben, the dark-clad immortal in the corner; others pointedly did not look at him. Ben watched every shift and every fidget, waiting to see how Jae approached the questions.

"Thank you all for coming," the human said. "I am sure you have heard of the tragic death of your fellow villager, Xi Haitao."

The men all nodded, keeping their eyes on Jae but surreptitiously glancing at each other as well.

"We are here because there was some evidence in his house that a woodworker had been there recently. Fresh pieces of wood, like from a small chisel or a drill."

Jae didn't mention that the wood was found *in* the blood. Smart. Ben was curious what the humans would assume.

A burly man in a green canvas jacket spoke up. "We all had business with Haitao; there are only two harness makers in the village, and his work was the best. I think we've all been to his house in the past few months to order some work."

"I have," another man said. "I was there last week."

Another man added, "I picked up a saddle for my horse last month, but I haven't been to his shop since then. And according to my wife, I leave sawdust wherever I go."

One man chuckled a little, and the rest of them murmured in agreement.

Jae was quick to respond. "We are not accusing any of you, of course, but all of you had accounts with Haitao and we wondered if there was anything you might be able to tell us about him that could help find the one who did this horrible thing. We asked at the tavern, and he wasn't known to have friends he drank with there. He had no family, so we are asking those who had business with him."

One of the quieter men asked, "Forgive me, brother, but we assumed..." His eyes darted to Ben. "I am sure there was a reason, of course, but was Haitao not killed by one of the Lǎoshī?"

"Why would you assume that?" Jae asked.

"I do not question it" —the man continued quickly— "but who else could do this thing?"

"That's why we're here." Ben spoke quietly from the corner. "We should assume nothing."

There was silence around the table for a few long moments.

"I had a fight with the bastard." A barrel-chested man with a quilted grey jacket and a scarred face spoke. "It was months ago, and I had nothing to do with his death, but I'm not going to pretend as if Haitao was liked." His voice was gruff and angry. "He discovered some embarrassing information about my wife, and he tried to force her to pay him money to keep it quiet. She was ashamed and was going to pay him until I found out. We fought. He decided to leave her alone, so I didn't report him to the magistrate, but who does that?" The man looked around at the other men. "It is not decent."

Three of the men looked shocked, but two of them didn't show any surprise.

Ben's interest was piqued.

So Haitao was a blackmailer. The man hadn't come right out and called it that, but if the harness maker had snooped around and tried to get money for one person's secrets, it was possible—likely even—that he'd done it to someone else too.

Ben was watching all the suspects, but his gaze had come to focus on one—a burly, dark-haired man who hadn't said a word after he gave Tai his name.

The human in front of him, listed as Le Tianyu in the building records, was a carpenter on the restoration of the Pearl Gate. His specialty was fine finishing work, like the intricate fretwork around the Pearl Seal, and his horse had been the one whose harness had snapped and caused the varnish spill.

Le Tianyu stared at the cup of tea nestled between his hands, avoiding Jae's eyes, avoiding Ben.

Ben walked over and sat at the other end of the table. "If

Haitao was threatening any of you, that could have led to a fight. Sometimes fights become more violent than we intend." He pushed sympathy and understanding into his voice. "It's better to be honest about an accident than try to conceal it."

"Why are you looking at us?" The gruff man spoke again. "So there was sawdust at the scene. There are a hundred ways it could have gotten there, and who knows how long it had been—"

"The sawdust was found in Haitao's blood." Jae leaned forward, leaning his elbows on the table. "Dropped there after he was dead."

The silence at the table was tangible.

"What do you say?" Ben looked from one man to the next. "Do any of you have a reasonable explanation for how fresh wood chips might have fallen into the harness maker's blood unless they were left there by his killer?"

"Probably the wind." It was Tianyu who spoke. He cleared his throat and continued. "The wood chips could have been anywhere, and then the wind might have blown them into his blood." He shrugged. "That's what I think anyway."

The man in the blue jacket laughed. "Tianyu, don't be foolish. Who would keep their windows open in the winter?"

Tianyu froze, and his eyes turned to Ben.

GOTCHA.

.   .   .

MAYBE THE WIND *HAD* BLOWN THE SAWDUST INTO THE blood. It was a perfectly reasonable explanation, but only if Tianyu had been there that night and knew that Haitao's windows had been wide open to the cold winter breeze.

———

TENZIN SAT IN SILENCE ON A LOW SILK COUCH IN THE anteroom of Sina's quarters in Elder Han's section of the palace compound as the ancient kept her waiting.

And waiting.

She'd already received a note from Ben that a suspect in the harness maker's killing had been identified, but she'd heard nothing since, and Zhang had left her to report their findings in the treasury to Elder Cao. It would be essential that they quietly find where the missing artifacts were and how they'd been stolen.

"Mistress Tenzin?"

Tenzin looked up and saw a servant standing in an arched doorway. "Yes?"

"Sina will see you now."

She rose and followed the servant into a hallway and to a pair of double doors. The servant opened the right side and ushered Tenzin into a room that had the same sweltering heat and humidity of the first chamber where she and Ben had met with the Pacific ancient.

Sina was sitting on a low woven cushion behind a tea table with two human women lounging behind her on silk couches. She looked up from a stack of papers and waved Tenzin over, motioning to another cushion across from her.

171

Tenzin sat and prepared to wait some more.

"Your mate is not with you." Sina made the statement without looking up from the table where Tenzin could see letters spread out, and another vampire was writing with an old-fashioned fountain pen and brilliant blue ink.

"He is not. He is questioning suspects in the town about the events of last night."

"Is this about my pearl?"

No, it's about a dead human. "We believe there was a murder in the town that may have had something to do with the theft, yes."

Sina looked up and set her fountain pen down. "A murder?"

"Yes. A harness maker who had been hired by some of the workers on the Pearl Gate renovation was killed. According to my partner, he was a blackmailer and may have discovered the identity of the thief."

"So the thief killed him?"

"It's possible."

"Hmm." Sina appeared interested. "You call him your partner, not your mate?"

Tenzin sensed that she should be careful with her words. Sina was an unknown. There was little Tenzin had even heard from rumors. She truly was a mystery, both intriguing and dangerous.

"Benjamin is both my mate and my partner."

Sina looked Tenzin up and down in a speculative sweep of her dark brown eyes. "Are you monogamous in your habits?"

In another time and another life, Tenzin would have been

more than interested. Everything that made Sina intriguing and dangerous made her attractive as well. Plus she was a beautifully formed woman. Her breasts were small and high set. Her lips were wide and full. Her skin glowed with life and warmth despite her element.

Tenzin smiled in appreciation of the compliment. "With my mate, I am monogamous, yes."

Sina lifted an eyebrow. "He is young."

"And possessive."

Sina pressed her lips forward in a thoughtful pout. "My mate and I are excellent allies and his element complements mine, but we are not monogamous. We have been mated for over a thousand years and prefer some variety in sexual partners."

"A thousand years is a long time."

"With luck, you will discover that yourself." Sina looked down again, picked up her pen, then swiped what looked like a signature over the bottom of the page and handed the letter to one of the women behind her, who took it from her fingers and scurried off. "The journey from our island takes some time. I had correspondence to catch up on. Thank you for your patience."

"I understood that Mahina handled the day-to-day running of your court?"

"We are in transition now, are we not?" Sina's lips offered a hint of a smile. "My daughter and her mate have come to me and told me of their wishes. It is not unreasonable, and my daughter is more than wise. Her son is ready to act as regent for a time." Sina looked down, picked up her pen again, and started another letter. "But that letter wasn't a business matter; it was for one of my children."

"Do you have many?"

"Yes."

"My lady—"

"Please, only call me Sina or Rumak. Name or title is all I need from those not my children."

"Sina then. I am happy for Elder Han's sake and for the benefit of Penglai Palace that Mahina will be able to reside here as much as she wishes. She can only bring prestige and wisdom to the court of the elders."

Sina didn't stop writing. "You are fortunate to have her. Find her pearl, or I will be forced to be insulted by the incompetence of the palace guard."

Tenzin bit her lip because she couldn't argue with her. The palace had become too casual about security. "The problem may be more complicated than one missing pearl."

The ancient looked up, and a gold loc fell from the twisted crown on her head. "Explain."

"I have recently examined the treasury," Tenzin said. "Can you tell me why three of the official state gifts you have given the elders over the past thousand years might have been stolen?"

Chapter Nineteen

Le Tianyu was rocking back and forth on a wooden stool in the small house where he lived. The front room was far neater than Haitao's and showed the touch of a woman, though no wife appeared when Ben and Jae appeared at the door. Instead, with a look of resignation, the carpenter ushered them in, brought two stools around the tea table in the living room, and started boiling water.

There was a delicacy and artistry to the home that was lacking in most other cottages in the village. There were exquisite, colorful paintings hanging on the walls, with hand-carved wood frames that were works of art in themselves.

The human's house screamed domestic comfort and family warmth. Books were stacked everywhere, and a doll was propped carefully in the corner with a yellow ribbon in its hair. A neat orange coat with pink trim hung by Tianyu's heavy work jacket.

"You live alone?" Ben asked.

The man kept his eyes on the steaming kettle. "No, my daughter lives with me."

Any child would be sleeping; it was near midnight.

Le Tianyu had a gentle demeanor, and nothing about him seemed capable of violence. Instead, the hands that poured boiling water into the teapot appeared deft and deliberate despite the calluses that marked him as a man of labor.

Jae whispered, "I never would have suspected him of murder."

"I still don't."

"Then what are we doing here?"

Ben murmured, "Because he knows something."

Tianyu brought the tea to the low table in the sitting area. "My wife died several years ago; she was an artist at the palace." He pointed to a childish painting of a woman in an intricately carved frame. "My daughter painted that just after she died. If she had a photograph, she would be able to make a better portrait now, but photographs are not allowed on the islands." He looked at the picture again. "She was very young when she made it."

"It's still *very* good." Ben was impressed. Clearly artistic talent ran in the family. "And you made the frame." Looking around the room, Ben saw more woodwork: beautifully made carvings, walking sticks with traditional motifs, and furniture that glowed with a flawless finish. "You're very talented."

Tianyu bowed. "Thank you. I only hope my talent can serve the elders. It is my honor to take care of their palace and keep it as beautiful and immortal as they are."

"But you did more at the Pearl Gate," Ben said. "Didn't you?"

Tianyu froze. "I don't know what you mean."

"Myung's records show that he chose you to be the head of the project, restoring the gate for Mistress Mahina's visit. You were in charge of the other carpenters."

Tianyu nodded. "Yes, I was head of the project."

Ben asked, "And you worked on the Pearl Seal yourself?"

The man swallowed. "I did."

"The jade and the gold wouldn't have needed to be more than cleaned, so I'm assuming you were the one who removed the seal to restore or remake the carved fretwork that made up the frame."

The man spoke in a quiet voice. "It was too damaged from the salt air. I had to remake it from scratch."

"Which is why it looked so flawless when the seal went missing, isn't that right?" Ben was sure of it. He didn't need to use amnis, as he'd been planning to do if the human resisted. "You restored the Pearl Seal; then you came back later and removed the gold dragon from the frame."

Tianyu didn't deny it. He didn't confirm. He appeared frozen, his large shoulders and shaggy head locked in a hunched position even though Ben could hear his heart pounding.

Jae stood. "Speak. Answer the elder's son."

"My daughter will be alone." The man stared at his large, callused hands. "Please, can you make sure someone takes care of my daughter? She is not like other children."

Jae barked at him. "What does Elder Zhang's son care about your daughter?" He was furious. "Tell us what you did with the Pearl Seal. You have shamed every human of Penglai

Island, shamed the elders you were meant to serve. Tell us where it is!"

Tianyu looked up and met Ben's eyes. "I never wanted to shame anyone. The shame is mine alone. Will you protect my daughter? If I tell you where it is, can you protect her? I told him Haitao had discovered me, but I didn't want... that. Now I am afraid. My daughter isn't like other children; I only took the seal because she doesn't belong here. There is nothing for her here, and I wanted to get her someplace—"

"Old man!" Jae towered over Tianyu. "What are you talking about? Tell us where the Pearl Seal is!"

A tapping sound came at the inner door, and Jae and Tianyu froze. Ben waited for someone to answer it, but no one moved. He stood, walked to the door, and opened it.

"Oh." The sight brought Ben an immediate smile. "Hello there."

A small face with round cheeks and sleepy eyes looked up but said nothing in return. It was a girl, maybe six or seven years old, with long black hair braided down her back, a yellow nightshirt, and slippers with cat ears.

Silently she walked across the room and crawled in her father's lap. Then she motioned with her hands, her small eyebrows drawn into one line.

Her father motioned back with one hand as the other held the little girl.

She couldn't hear. Tianyu had a daughter, and she could not hear or speak.

Pieces of a puzzle started falling into place.

The islanders' lives haven't changed in hundreds of years.

Everyone has their role on the islands. Everyone has a place...

She is not like other children.

She doesn't belong here.

Ben walked back to the living area, sat on the stool, and watched Tianyu with his little girl, a little girl who clearly needed something she could not get on an island run by ancient vampires who hadn't changed in hundreds of years.

"You stole the Pearl Seal to get your daughter off the island," Ben said. "Someone told you that if you stole it, they could get you and your daughter to the mainland."

Tianyu rocked his daughter gently; the little girl had already fallen asleep in her father's safe arms. "He told me there were schools for children like Jiayi in the city of Shanghai. That there were other children like her. He believed me when I told him she was just as smart—smarter even—than other children. That she could do more if the school was willing to teach her. She is even more talented than Shuang was—her mother. But she is bright as well as talented. She could learn if someone would teach her. The school here says there is no point, but I know she could learn."

"Where is the seal? Do you still have it?"

Tianyu nodded. "I hid it. He said I had to keep it with me until it was time. I don't know how Haitao found out that I had taken it, but he threatened to tell the town guard." He glanced down to make sure his daughter was sleeping. "I didn't know what to do," he whispered. "I was going to his house to pay him, but I found him dead."

"Who was it?" Ben leaned forward. "Who told you to take the Pearl Seal?"

———

TENZIN HATED TALKING ON THE PHONE. IF THERE WAS one thing she appreciated about modern life, it was the ability to video chat. Well, that and YouTube. She loved watching videos about how industrial machines operated, how robots were made, and funny videos with cats and dogs. And ducks.

What she didn't like was talking to people when she couldn't see their face.

But since no modern devices were allowed on Penglai, she was forced to use the forty-year-old landline in the communications room on the island. It was a soundproofed room that wasn't all that soundproof, and it contained a single rotary phone that couldn't be shorted out, not even by the volatile fire vampires.

"Jonathan?"

"Who is this? Tenzin?"

"Yes, it's me."

"Why do you sound as if you're calling from the year 1958?"

"Because that's probably when this phone was made."

"Good God, are you still on Penglai? Whatever happened with the Pearl Seal? I thought you and Ben would be long gone by now."

Tenzin huffed. "I can't ask or answer anything if you keep talking."

"Fine."

They both sat in silence for a good while.

"Are you going to speak?" Jonathan asked.

"I wanted to make sure you were done."

"Tenzin, just ask me what you want to ask me and be done with it." Jonathan was clearly getting annoyed. "Believe it or not, I actually do have to work tonight."

Tenzin smiled. She did enjoy irritating Jonathan.

"I need to know about grain shipments from Australia," she said. "According to the shipping records here, your boats have been taking grain from Australia to Beijing. Was any of it wheat?"

"Are you saying the elders are keeping track of what Cheng ships?"

"Are you surprised?"

"I— Never mind. Wheat? Of course we ship wheat," Jonathan said. "We handle quite a lot of it. The Chinese market in the north is voracious."

"What about organic old wheat?" Tenzin asked.

"Old wheat?"

"Old varieties of wheat. Things the big farms don't grow anymore."

"I would have to look up exact numbers to be sure, but artisanal varieties of wheat are generally more expensive, and organic always fetches a better price than conventional crops."

"How much more?"

"For organic? I would estimate a third higher. For organic and rare varieties of wheat? Easily twice as much as conventional."

Twice as much? That was more than a little interesting.

"Tenzin, why are you asking—?"

"Thank you." She hung up.

So organic wheat fetched a much better price than the

human varieties they grew on big farms, and there were useless shipments of wheat in the storehouse at the monastery.

Three pallets, in fact.

Three.

She'd been quietly judging Ben for his interest in the wheat production on the islands, but she finally understood why it had bothered him. It all tied together: human life on the islands, the theft of the seal, the labyrinthine shipping patterns from the outer islands to the main island to the mainland.

It was meant to be confusing; it had been set up that way.

All to conceal a dripping embezzlement that had the added benefit of causing the Eight Immortals to lose face and possibly create a rift in their South Pacific alliance.

It was time to find Ben; she just hoped he'd managed to narrow down the human suspects. When it came to the vampire ones? She only had one name in her mind.

Chapter Twenty

The great hall was as full the next night as it had been on the night of Mahina and Sina's reception. Officially, it was the welcome banquet for Sina and her delegation.

Unofficially, Ben and Tenzin had other plans.

The elders were on their thrones with their immortal offspring in attendance along with their staff, human and vampire.

All told, the hall was standing room only. While Ben and Tenzin were near the front of the room with Elder Zhang before them, they were still packed shoulder to shoulder with other immortals, which was both irritating and dangerous. Humans, except for a rare few near the elders, were lined up in the back.

Ben kept his voice low. "Do you think they plan these things to be recipes for violence?"

"No, but they're oblivious to the threat of it." She looked over to Lu Dongbin's section. "He's here."

"Of course he is. If he wasn't, it would look suspicious."

"You have it?"

"Yes, and it's heavy."

Tenzin switched from Mandarin to Spanish. "I still think we should have made a replica and kept it."

"How on earth did you plan on finding a pearl that could possibly replicate Mahina's Eye?"

"I don't think Sina would notice."

"I think you're delusional." Ben glanced around the room. "Why are there so many humans here?"

Tenzin frowned, and it was one of those moments where Ben felt as if he were about twelve years old.

"It's a banquet, Benjamin."

"You mean...?"

"Yes." She nodded. "There are many vampires here, and they will need to feed."

Ben barely stopped the wince. "Publicly?"

"Probably not, but it's a little bit like having a full table displayed at a reception. Knowing the humans are there to feed from should calm down any vampires who feel a bit growly."

"I am so not telling any of the people here you compared them to a buffet." Ben looked to the right where Sina's delegation—including Mahina—had been positioned near Elder Han's throne so they could look over the crowd as well as the elders. The dais was long and decorated with flowers, beautifully dyed cloth, and silk-covered furniture.

Mahina appeared to be conferring quietly with any number of people who came and went while Sina looked bored. Her lips were pushed forward in a slight pout, and her shoulders were slumped.

He leaned down. "I still can't figure Sina out."

"Don't try." Tenzin stepped forward, walked up the steps, and whispered something to Elder Zhang. Zhang gave a nod to Elder Lu Dongbin, who rose to his feet.

"Honored guests, visiting regents." He nodded at Sina. "Thank you for joining us tonight for this banquet, welcome feast, and reception for our honored guests from the south."

Guests in Penglai didn't clap, but there were satisfied whispers around the room.

Elder Lu continued. "In addition to introducing our guests, we will also be introducing a new resident of Penglai tonight."

Mahina stood and turned to look at Elder Han.

For a moment Ben forgot about the cold metal against his torso, the betrayal of the island, and the murder of the human who'd been in the way. He looked at Elder Han and Mahina, both their faces reflecting a quiet joy that felt tangible in the room.

Ben reached for Tenzin's hand and wove her fingers between his.

Sina stood and addressed Elder Lu. "Honored Elders of Penglai, my daughter Mahina, daughter of the great Tanifa, chief of the Heilala Throne, and most beloved of all my children has asked my leave to join her mate, the most esteemed Elder Han Xiang of the southern waters, at his residence here on Penglai Island."

Though the news wasn't news to Ben and Tenzin, it

apparently was to many in the audience because a murmur of surprise drifted across the room.

"It doesn't sound negative," Ben said. "But... cautious?"

"I think that's a good summation." Tenzin craned her neck to see Sina. "She didn't exactly phrase it as a question."

The corner of Ben's mouth lifted. "I have a feeling it wasn't a question."

Elder Lu Dongbin addressed Sina. "Honored Sina, we welcome Mahina, mate of Elder Han and holder of the Heilala Throne to her place at Elder Han's side. Further, we express our gratitude that her wisdom and experience will be added to the hall of the elders."

A wooden throne carved with delicate flowers was brought out and placed at the bottom of the front dais, a seat of honor but not on par with the elders', a signal that while Mahina would be joining her mate, she would not be a ninth elder or have the same status.

Mahina's face revealed nothing as she turned to her sire. Ben could see a silent exchange between them before Mahina stepped down from her sire's platform, walked across the hall, and took her seat in front of her mate.

"It's a demotion," Ben whispered.

"Yes." Tenzin squeezed his hand. "But it must be one she sought. The weight of leadership is heavy, and perhaps she wanted a rest."

He looked at her. "This is why you never want to take Zhang's place."

"No." She looked up. "Careful. He might try to convince you, and if you think I'll be willing to sit anywhere near you if you take that job, you're fooling yourself."

Ben smiled. "Noted."

"Are you ready?"

Ben turned and saw Elder Zhang looking in his direction.

This was the part he'd been dreading. He'd never liked the spotlight, and this was a spotlight like no other in the immortal world.

He stepped forward, retrieving a large circular object wrapped in silk from the interior of his formal coat. He walked past Elder Zhang, Elder Cao, Elder He, and Elder Lu, and he was just halfway across the hall. He passed Elder Zhongli, Elder Li, and Elder Lan before he finally made it to Elder Han and the beautiful vampire he was privileged to call his mate.

Ben bowed deeply. "Mistress Mahina, as the son of Elder Zhang, eldest of the Eight Immortals, I am honored to return to you the Eye of Mahina and the Pearl Seal."

He placed the red silk wrapping on her knees and watched as Mahina's eyes lit in delight. "Benjamin, son of Zhang, I thank you for returning this precious treasure to me and my mate."

Ben walked back across the hall, silence following every step, and he couldn't help but cast his eyes toward Myung.

The vampire's jaw was tight, his lips couldn't conceal his fangs, and his eyes were locked on Ben.

———

AFTER THE PRESENTATION OF THE SEAL, THE HALL WAS cleared and vampire and human guests were ushered into the garden where long tables were set out with huge platters of food, bottles of blood-wine, and various delicacies designed for light vampire appetites.

As Ben had suspected, he saw various immortals sneaking off to the shadows with humans in tow, eager to partake of more private sustenance. Still, the garden was filled with chatter, music from traditional musicians, and dancers who moved gracefully in the flickering torchlight.

Ben and Tenzin stood on the edge of the gathering, watching the festivities and keeping their eyes on Myung, who was stationed at a table with two human men on either side.

Sina's table was centered in the garden, and she must have been told who had taken the Pearl Seal, because her eyes were locked on Myung.

"That doesn't look good," Ben said.

"She knows it's not her place to take action," Tenzin said. "But someone must."

Zhang approached them from behind. "Benjamin. Tenzin. The return of the Pearl Seal was excellently done. You have done the island a service."

Ben pointed his chin toward Myung. "And him?"

Zhang's mouth fell into a flat line. "The elders have decided that a quiet resolution should suffice in this matter."

Tenzin scoffed. "Saving face again?"

Zhang cocked his head. "Exposing Myung's theft publicly might satisfy your desire for vengeance, daughter, but it does nothing to bring honor to any of the parties wronged."

"You say quiet resolution, and I say covering up the sins of an elder."

After careful questioning at the monastery and in the village, Ben and Tenzin had reported to the elders that they believed Myung had not only worked with an accomplice to steal the Pearl Seal but the other treasures missing from the island as well. He then shipped them out with excess grain shipments sent directly from the farming islands to the mainland. Wheat and barley were leaving the islands, and the profit went into Myung's own pocket.

"Elder Lu says he had no idea of Myung's betrayal," Zhang said, "and I believe him. He has no reason to lie."

"And Elder Cao? His children are in charge of the treasury."

"All these questions will be sorted with patience and time. Making a spectacle does nothing to bring the island back into balance."

Ben listened to their quiet argument, but he couldn't help but notice a dozen men in traditional armor take positions along the edge of the garden.

"Lu has every reason to lie if he was part of it. His son was stealing food from the people and gold from the elders." Tenzin turned to Ben. "I want to leave. Tonight."

The guards took a step forward, still in silent formation.

Then another.

"Tiny—"

"Myung stole sacred relics, killed a human, and terrorized a family who served this island for generations." Tenzin pointed to the vampire's table. "I would kill him myself with one blow, yet there he sits, drinking blood-wine and—"

"Killing him would do nothing and will not lead us to his conspirators. If there are more vampires involved—"

189

"That's an excuse."

"Tiny."

She turned to Ben in fury. "You, of all people, I thought would understand—"

"Lu's guards are taking him," Ben said quietly. "Right now."

She turned and saw what Ben had been seeing.

Elder Lu Dongbin's guards were narrowing in on the table. No one seemed to notice what was happening except for Myung, Ben and Tenzin, and the elders, all of whom had their eyes fixed on the betrayer.

Myung sat frozen for a moment, seemingly resigned to the soldiers coming for him; then he shot to his feet, drew two swords from the folds of his robe, and spun, hacking off the heads of the two humans sitting with him and rotating in a whirl toward the guard as blood-sprayed humans began to scream and flee the garden.

Among Lu's guard were water vampires who lifted their arms and commanded the torrents coming from the fountains to surround their prey, but Myung was a water vampire too, and Elder Lu's own son. He swept the wall of water away with one arm, lunging toward an armored guard and stabbing him through the neck with one swift blow.

Within seconds, the delicately balanced elements of the immortal garden of the elders became a battleground of those same elements.

Chapter Twenty-One

"I t's not just Myung!" Ben took to the air with Tenzin following him. "Look, he's got help."

It wasn't only Myung fighting Lu's guard. An earth vampire in Elder Cao's household and a wind vampire from Elder Zhongli's guard had taken up the fallen dao of the guards Myung had killed. The wind vampire was attacking from above, and while humans ran, he picked up one of the dancers and threw her across the garden toward Sina's table.

Ben yelled, "Tenzin!"

"Got her!" Tenzin raced through the air in a blur, catching the young woman and setting her on the ground before she joined Ben in the air.

The wind vampire stopped his attacks on humans and twisted his arm to form a tornado that touched down on the water Lu's guards were still using to attack Myung. He spun it out of their reach, flinging the mist into the night sky.

Ben glanced at the ground and saw the elders standing on

the steps of the hall, not a single one lifting a hand to quell the chaos ensuing below.

"What are they doing?" Ben shouted.

"They have taken vows of peace," Tenzin said. "None of them can fight publicly. Not like this."

Ben spotted Jae racing toward a group of humans who had been pulled into the earth up to the waist. Fissures had formed in the garden as the earth vampire ripped open the ground and caught humans and the vampires who were trying to fight them.

The human guards were busy trying to rescue the mortal partygoers from the chaos Myung and his allies had created while the vampire guard was scattered, protecting the elders and the vampire guests while the elders looked on.

"This is ridiculous." Ben felt like spitting. "There are only three of them. No one is going to help?"

Tenzin turned to Ben. "I'll take care of Elder Cao's son and the other." She flew toward him and pressed a hard kiss to his lips. "You end Myung."

"Weapons?"

Tenzin smiled and drew one of Ben's favorite curved sabers from the voluminous robe she'd worn to dinner.

Ben grinned. "I love you."

"I know." With a wicked gleam in her eye, she produced a katar from one pocket and an arm-length scimitar from another.

"Where...?" Ben shook his head. "I probably don't want to know."

Tenzin held the punch dagger in her left hand, the scimitar in her right, and drifted backward toward the tornado. "Happy hunting, Benjamin."

Ben felt a burst of bloodlust in his veins and knew that while part of what he was feeling was Tenzin's thirst for battle, he was also feeling his own. Myung was a skilled warrior, and three human guards had joined him along with his two vampire conspirators. They weren't going to win, but they were doing an admirable job of causing chaos among the mortals before they died.

End this. End Myung.

Ben arrowed himself toward the water vampire, whose back was against a scholar's stone where a dancing fountain had once filled their air with tranquility. Now Myung was using the water like spears, one arm slicing through the air, guiding the water that cut the guards who approached him with razor-sharp edges while he battled another vampire who was carrying a ceremonial spear.

He was old, the son of an elder, and far more powerful than Ben had realized.

"Myung!"

The water vampire turned toward the sound of his voice and Ben reached out, wrapped the air around Myung's water, and yanked hard. The liquid spear shattered into mist as Ben shoved another wall of air toward it, pushing the water away from Myung and draining him of his element.

But Myung turned the water back and the mist enveloped Ben, dampening his amnis and pulling at his energy. They were on an island, the air was rich with the sea, and Myung was an experienced warrior. He dragged Ben to the ground with the force of the mist, but Ben wrested the air into his control and shoved it back. The skin of water that Myung had forced around him shivered and collapsed to the ground.

Ben took to the air again, arrowing toward Myung with his sword out. He wasted no energy on flourishes, aiming his blade directly at the vampire's neck, but Myung ducked out of the way and Ben's sword and shoulder scraped against the rugged limestone column.

"Stop this!" Ben shouted as Myung grabbed a sword from the fallen body of a human guard. "What do you think you're doing? You can't get away!"

The vampire said nothing but lunged toward Ben, aiming the tip of his blade at his throat. Ben shoved a hand out, and the air forced Myung's blade upward. The vampire stumbled but quickly regained his footing and twisted to the side, slicing the side of Ben's leg with one sweep.

Burning pain lanced up his left side, and he pulled his element to himself, lifting away from Myung's reach, into the air where the water vampire couldn't get to him.

Ben attacked from above, swooping down like a bird and slicing Myung over and over again, dodging his arrows of water, keeping him distracted from weaker foes.

He felt his mate in the distance, the hunger in her blood and the jolt of satisfaction when an enemy perished. He turned and looked for her, but she was battling in the clouds, keeping Myung's accomplices busy while Ben attacked the stronger opponent.

Myung had twin blades, and he swept through a clutch of human guards who charged him, leaving a chaos of blood, fallen bodies, and twisted limbs.

Ben felt helpless at the carnage. He was the son of Zhang, but Myung was the son of an elder too. Ben's amnis might have been more powerful, but Myung had centuries of experience, ruthless cunning, and nothing to lose. Myung was keeping him busy battling spears of water while he made his way toward the gates of the palace.

If he could get out of the walls and into the sea, he could escape, and then all this carnage would have been for nothing.

The air pressed close to him, whispering secrets and guiding the sound of Myung's grunts to his ears. The constant attacks were wearing on the water vampire, and Ben sensed a chink in his armor.

He closed his eyes and reached out with his amnis, his elemental sense breaching the distance between him and Myung. He felt the air within the water and the space within Myung.

Ben kept his eyes closed, and the image the wind whispered to him was the darkness in the world. He saw the earth below him like glowing gold riven with air. The water was a silver mist threaded with space, and the torches that surrounded the garden sucked the darkness in, transforming it into light.

He saw Myung in the middle of the chaos, a creature of gold and silver, of matter and fire, but within every particle of the immortal was the space that Ben recognized, the air that was within all things.

He pulled the darkness with his amnis and heard the strangled scream of anger before he snatched the air from

Myung's lungs and felt the breath within his enemy kiss his own lips.

———

TENZIN WATCHED WITH WIDE EYES, HER ENEMIES BOTH vanquished, their blood staining her lips. She gazed in amazement as Ben rose higher and higher in the sky and drew Myung to him, pulled as if Ben was drawing the air between them into himself.

The human guards on the ground gaped in amazement. The elders watched with keen interest. And Zhang?

Zhang was looking at her, a half smile gracing his lips.

You knew.

I knew.

Tenzin's eyes returned to her mate, and she fed his energy with her own.

He didn't need it.

She saw Myung rising from the ground, his body locked. The swords fell from his hands and clattered to the ground as Ben excised the space between them.

Her mate somehow appeared bigger, as if the matter that made him had expanded, grown, as his amnis pulled the air from Myung and added it to himself.

One day he will be infinite.

———

BEN OPENED HIS EYES, AND MYUNG WAS BEFORE HIM, floating in the air over the palace. He could feel Myung's element in the distance, batting at the space Ben controlled, like rain spitting on a metal roof.

Myung's eyes were pure hatred.

"Why?" Ben asked the vampire, who seemed to shrink before him moment by moment.

Myung opened his mouth, but nothing came out.

He can't speak.

Ben allowed air into the vampire's lungs.

"N-not a servant."

Ben glanced down at his sire, then at the other elders, then at Tenzin. His eyes returned to Myung. "We all serve."

The air whispered around him, the darkness caressing his face and asking him what he wanted.

"What did you want?"

Myung gasped for air and Ben allowed it.

"Money. Power. R-respect."

"You could have had all those things without stealing from the elders, without killing that man."

"Be..." He gasped and reached for his element, but there was nothing but what Ben allowed.

Space. He finally understood what it meant.

He allowed Myung more air.

"Be a servant for centuries and see how respected you feel."

Ben cocked his head and realized that Myung's shallow reasoning was the truth. He felt smaller by serving the elders. He used the humans on the island to make himself feel bigger. He stole from the treasury to see if he could. All of it.

All of it was because Myung himself felt small.

End him.

The wind whispered it, and Ben drew his sword back. It was the only end to a vampire who had manipulated so many and risked so much. He'd betrayed the elders, abused his power over the humans, to the point of murdering a man for threatening to expose his secrets.

Myung knew it was coming. "Finish it."

His eyes never changed. Hatred in darkest brown. Ben sliced his blade forward, cleanly separating Myung's head from his body.

The vampire's amnis, the energy that animated him in immortality, sighed and released. The body fell to the ground with a loud thud, and Ben released his hold on the air around them.

He heard a distant pop and floated down to the ground, reaching out for his mate.

Tenzin took his hand in her own, turned him, and pressed her palm to his cheek. She drew him down for a kiss, her hand never leaving his skin, and the blood and amnis within Ben centered and settled as the darkness within him leached away.

The wind died down, and it was just the two of them with the air around them dancing as the blood in the garden cooled.

Chapter Twenty-Two

The following night, Ben and Tenzin met with the elders, Sina, and Mahina in the elders' garden after the bodies in the palace had been given a proper burial by the daoshi, the blood had been turned into the soil by Elder Cao and Elder Li, and a heavy rain had washed the compound clean.

"We owe you a debt," Elder Lu said. "Both for the return of the seal and for exposing the conspiracy within our own palace."

Ben bowed slightly. "A friend told me once that long-established powers are not always able to see unrest within their own walls. With all respect, I believe Myung used your trust in him to take advantage."

Tenzin watched their reaction. It was a challenging statement for a young vampire to make, but no one who had witnessed Benjamin's display of power over the palace the night before could doubt that he was every bit as powerful as most of the elders anyway.

Ben hadn't just been a master of air in battle, he had bridled emptiness as few immortals ever did. He had an innate sense of space, a sense that had taken Tenzin centuries to even touch, but for him—and perhaps with the urging of her own blood in his—he had used not only his own air but the air within Myung to defeat him.

The Immortal Woman hadn't spoken much in either of their meetings with Ben and Tenzin but now said, "You never told us the name of the human thief. I assume you know which human took the Pearl Seal from its frame."

Ben looked at Tenzin, who stepped forward. "We do," she said. "But we will be taking care of the thief ourselves."

Tenzin would have to make it clear to Jae that he didn't need to include the name of the carpenter or his daughter in the official report. Both father and daughter were already out of the jurisdiction of the elders anyway. Tenzin had put them on a small boat that Jonathan had sent that afternoon. At that moment, Tianyu and his little girl were hundreds of kilometers away.

"Unacceptable," Elder Lu said. "We need to know the identity of the thief. Those who betray the elders must pay the price so that we can stamp out even the idea of disrespect."

It wasn't lost on anyone that Elder Lu's own son had been the one to betray them. Then again, he hadn't raised a finger to help his child, who had betrayed the island; and neither had Elder Cao, whose son had helped Myung steal from the treasury; or Elder Zhongli, from whose house the third conspirator hailed.

Zhang was the one who responded. "You have earned a

favor from the council. As Elder Lu said, a debt." He cocked his head. "Perhaps the identity of the thief is your favor."

"Elder Zhang—"

"I believe" —Zhang turned to his friend— "if my son or my daughter believed this individual a threat to the elders, they would turn the thief over to us." He looked at Ben and Tenzin. "But my children have proven to be faithful to their sire and his allies, have they not?"

"Indeed," Elder Han concurred. "Unless my mate or her sire have objections to Ben and Tenzin being put in charge of the human thief, I have no argument with allowing them to see to justice as they deem appropriate."

Everyone waited for Sina and Mahina to speak. The two water vampires exchanged probing looks before Mahina said, "My mate speaks for my mother and me. The Eye of Mahina and the Pearl Seal have been returned. The organizer of the plot is dead. We have no objection to this."

"Nor do I," Elder Cao said. "I only offer my regrets that a traitor came from my own blood." The sweet-faced elder's eyes were mournful. "And I will do everything possible to retrieve the valuables that were taken from the treasury."

"With all the traitors dead," Elder Zhang said, "it could be difficult."

"I have sources on the mainland," Elder Lan said, their lyrical voice speaking for the first time. "I believe I may know where Myung might have sold them." They spoke to Sina. "Don't worry, old friend."

"I am not worried," Sina said. "And the elders may be assured that I will be looking into any connections Ayal might have had with Elder Lu's son." She looked around the garden.

"A human thief is no concern of mine, but if Ayal was conspiring with Myung to interfere with our alliance" —her eyes moved to Han's— "you can be sure that I will discover it."

"Then the matter is finished." Elder Zhang turned to Ben and Tenzin. "You may leave."

Tenzin took Ben by the arm and led him out of the garden. "Let's go."

"Your bag is already packed, isn't it?" He sounded amused. "Seriously, Tiny?"

"He said we could leave." She was already floating over the garden. "And we're overdue for a holiday with presents."

Ben smiled. "And pretty lights in trees."

"Chocolate."

"And tamales."

Tenzin smiled. "I forgot about the tamales."

"How could you forget about the tamales?"

———

TIANYU COULDN'T HELP IT. HE WATCHED THE DARKNESS in the north, waiting for the lights of the island to rise.

"You won't be able to see them," the captain said. "We're already far too distant from Penglai to see a trace."

He was sitting on the deck of a wooden boat the captain kept calling a yacht, a magnificent vessel the likes of which Tianyu had never seen. They had watched the sunset over the mainland in the distance, and now his daughter was curled next to him, wrapped in the bright orange blanket her mother had loved.

Put her on the blanket, Xīngān. Look at her sweet face. She is so perfect. I'm going to draw a picture.

He frowned, thinking of the paintings they had to leave behind, the last of Shuang's clothes and her books. Other than her favorite dress, they hadn't had time to pack everything he wanted. Most of her paintings and all his woodcarvings had stayed behind. They'd taken everything from the small shrine in the house, but there was so much they'd had to leave at the cottage.

A new start. New memories.

Tianyu looked at the captain, who had introduced herself as Cristina. Jae, the palace guard, had taken them from their house in a covered horse cart to the far side of the island where they had boarded the boat in the shadow of the Pearl Gate and the elders' palace.

Tianyu felt a lightness in his chest. The accusing dragon was gone. They had been given papers that looked official and were being taken to the home of one of the vampires who had discovered them.

Cristina had assured Tianyu that he and Jiayi would be well taken care of, and she had given him a paper with many numbers on it. Her name was next to one of the numbers, then another one had an American name next to it and another bore the name Tenzin. They were numbers Tianyu could call on a telephone, though he had never used one. He knew what they were, but he'd only ever seen them used in the magistrate's office.

"Life is going to be very different," Captain Cristina said. "But you will adapt. And your carpentry skills are very much needed, especially in places like Shanghai where many people have boats."

"I have never built boats," Tianyu said. "That is a different trade."

"Have you built cabinets?" She asked. "How about furniture?"

"Of course."

She shrugged. "So you'll find work. I'm sure of it. Look inside this boat. All the cabinets and furnishings were made by a woodworker like you."

Tianyu craned his neck, but other than an initial tour, he'd kept mostly outside on the deck. Everything else felt overwhelming. He'd never once stepped off the islands other than onto a small ferry to go from one to the other, and now he was speeding through the ocean on a yacht, going to a place where he knew no one and no one knew him.

His eyes returned to Jiayi. "I was told there are schools for children like my daughter in Shanghai."

The captain's voice was soft. "I believe Tenzin's secretary has already called and arranged an interview for her."

"And they will be willing to teach her?"

"Yes. In fact, I'm pretty sure that eventually your daughter will be the one teaching you." Cristina laughed. "At least that's how my teenagers are with me."

Tianyu turned and met the captain's eyes. "You have children."

She nodded. "Two. So when I say you can trust me to get you and your daughter to safety, believe me." She shook her head. "Besides, as of right now, you're under the aegis of

Benjamin, son of Zhang, nephew of Giovanni Vecchio. Trust me, no one is going to mess with you."

Tianyu didn't know the foreign name the captain mentioned, but he knew Zhang and he knew the serious, dark-haired wind vampire who had discovered his crime. Something in his heart had told him he could confide in that vampire, and so far it seemed that fate had been kind.

"As long as Jiayi will have a better life," Tianyu said. "I will go anywhere."

Chapter Twenty-Three

Ben sat beside the Christmas tree as Sadia, his little sister, opened her present from Tenzin.

His little sister gasped, and he could feel, rather than hear, her parents' unspoken groans.

"Tenzin, you didn't," Giovanni muttered.

"Seriously?" Beatrice put a hand over her eyes.

"You got me a *katar*?" Sadia hugged the Indian punch dagger to her chest. It was in a beautifully worked leather sheath, but Ben still tensed. "Is it sharp?"

Tenzin frowned. "Of course it is. Why would I give you a dull dagger?"

Sadia let out a squeal of the type that only an almost-eight-year-old girl could make.

In fact, Ben was pretty sure his mate had given his little sister the same dagger she'd recently used to kill two vampires in Penglai, but he wasn't going to say anything to Sadia's parents about that. After all, Tenzin was meticulous about cleaning her weapons, and the katar was a particularly nice specimen.

Sadia threw her arms around Tenzin. "I love it! I love it so much."

"I'm glad." Tenzin patted Sadia's back. "You're still too young for sword training, but it will be a nice start for a serious collection. Until you're a bit older, I'm sure your mother can keep it in her sword safe for you."

"Okay." His sister looked at Tenzin with stars in her eyes. "I'll take such good care of it; I promise."

"I know you will; otherwise, I wouldn't have given it to you." Tenzin turned to Beatrice. "You know just recently, that dagger came in very handy when—"

"I think it's time for the next present!" Ben nearly shouted. "Or panettone? Did someone make panettone this year?"

"I think it's the perfect time for panettone," Giovanni said. "Ben, why don't you and I go get the sweet bread while Beatrice and Tenzin finish presents with Sadia?"

"Sounds good." He caught Tenzin's eye and mouthed, *No stories.*

She shrugged. *What?*

Ben followed his uncle into the kitchen and walked directly to the breadboard where a beautifully golden loaf of bread sat, pocked with candied fruit and wrapped in parchment paper.

"Okay, I don't know who baked that—"

"If I need to inspect that weapon for bodily fluids or gore, you need to tell me now," Giovanni said quickly.

"I'm sure she cleaned it," Ben said. "But... maybe check, just to be sure."

He rolled his eyes and shook his head. "Tenzin."

"I mean, you're not really surprised, are you?"

"No." He glanced over his shoulder at Ben as he unwrapped the panettone and brought it to the cutting board. "How were the islands?"

"The elders were fine." Ben grabbed five small plates and set them on the counter, then leaned against it and watched his uncle cut the bread. "I believe I left Zhang with some ideas for educational reform that he hadn't considered in a few thousand years, so I'll take that as a win."

Giovanni said, "It's not a place that's prone to change."

"We have a new employee at the house in Shanghai," Ben said quietly. "They... uh... It's a father and daughter from Penglai. They needed to leave, so I put them under... I mean, they needed protection, so..."

Giovanni slowly turned. "You put them under *your* aegis?"

It felt strange even to say it. His uncle had humans under aegis. Zhang had humans under aegis. Tenzin even had a very few. Aegis was a powerful relationship, a role of formal protection. An umbrella that told the human that—in the vampire world—that vampire would protect them.

"I didn't do it lightly," Ben said. "But it was complicated and they needed a new start. It was this guy and his little girl. They didn't have anyone—"

"You're ready." Giovanni walked over and put a hand on his shoulder. "Ben, you're ready for that responsibility. I know who you are, and you're ready."

"Thank you." Giovanni might not be his biological father, but he'd been the one to teach Ben what it was to be a man. "I'll protect them."

"I have no doubt you will." He walked back to the cutting board and began putting fat slices of sweet bread on the small plates Ben had set out. "There have been rumors about you, even here."

"About me?"

"About the power you exhibited in Penglai," Giovanni said. "Amnis isn't supposed to work on vampires, you know."

"It's not the amnis," Ben said. "It's that..." How could he explain? "If I close my eyes now and look at you, my amnis would show me you, but... *not* you."

Giovanni frowned. "Explain more."

"I can see the elements. Gold matter, silver water, the red fire that eats everything and spits it out again transformed. But the space between everything is dark, Gio. The space between all things... It's beautiful, and that space feels like it's mine, you know?" He put a hand to his chest. "I can see it. And feel it. And... manipulate it."

Giovanni stared at him. "You can see the space between earth and water, and that's what you can manipulate?"

"I can feel it the same way you feel fire. The same way that B can feel water." Ben shrugged. "I don't know how, I just can."

"You're talking about amnis at an atomic level, Ben." He looked at the ground, then up again. "There are those who will consider it a threat."

"I know. I wasn't thinking. I just knew I needed to stop Myung, so I did."

Giovanni nodded slowly. "Then you'll handle it. Whatever comes. You'll handle it with Tenzin beside you." He let out a slow breath. "I love you, and I can't imagine a better mate by your side. The two of you... It was meant to be. Everything in your life confirms it."

Ben closed his eyes. "Please, for the love of God, don't tell her that. Her ego is already out of control."

Giovanni laughed and picked up a plate of sweet bread.

"Thank you."

He turned to Ben. "For what?"

Ben shrugged. "Just for everything."

His uncle smiled. "Good thing I gave that little pickpocket a chance to prove himself."

"Yeah." He smiled a little. "Sometimes all a thief needs is a second chance. To make something of himself. To make something new."

Giovanni handed Ben a plate of bread. "And don't forget: everyone needs something sweet of their own to look forward to."

Ben thought about his sister squealing over sharp objects, his aunt desperately trying to lock up her sword collection, and his mate who gleefully fed the madness.

Ben pressed his lips together to keep the laugh from escaping. "I don't know if I'd call them traditionally sweet, but... they're definitely ours."

———

Thank you for reading Ben and Tenzin's newest adventure! I promise, there will be more in the future.

Pearl Sky

If you haven't experienced the Elemental Covenant series, you can find more information on my website. The next paranormal mystery featuring Brigid and Carwyn is BISHOP'S FLIGHT, coming Summer 2023.

And for more information about all my work, please visit, ElizabethHunterWrites.com.

Look inside: Paladin's Kiss

Enjoy this preview of the Elemental Covenant series!
Saint's Passage, Martyr's Promise, and Paladin's
Kiss now available at all major retailers in ebook, audiobook,
and paperback.

B rigid saw the flashing blue lights in the side mirror, and her fangs dropped. She turned to her husband, who was driving the van. "I told ya it was a speed trap."

Carwyn glanced to the side, then at the rearview mirror. "I was barely over the limit." He pulled over onto the rough gravel shoulder. "I'll do the talking, wife. You have a habit of rankling law enforcement."

Brigid glanced at the three unconscious humans in the back of their converted Volkswagen van. "Can't imagine why."

The back of her throat burned when she smelled the humans behind their vehicle. The men passed out behind her stank of alcohol, methamphetamines, and sour sweat. It was easy to ignore their scent, but the officers behind them?

They smelled like dinner.

"He's sitting on the hood of his car," Carwyn muttered. "No respect for the schedule of others."

"It's a tactic to make us nervous." Brigid narrowed her eyes as she watched her side mirror. "They definitely think we're carrying drugs. Second one out of the car."

"A camper van with California plates driving through rural Louisiana in the middle of the night?" Carwyn smiled as the man who'd been perched on the hood of the cruiser started to walk toward them. "I can't imagine why they'd think drugs were an issue."

She cranked down the van window and saw the outline of a second officer eyeing her window with interest in the flashing lights from the other side of the police cruiser.

"Tá dhá cheann acu." *There are two of them.* She spoke in Irish, unwilling to give any information to the humans. "Second one is staying back."

Carwyn glanced in the mirror. "Noted."

"Má chuardaíonn said an carr..." *If they search the car...*

"They won't." He was wearing a black button-down shirt dotted with bloodstains. He carefully buttoned it up to the neck.

Brigid frowned. "What are you doing?"

He quickly folded a receipt and stuck it in a cup holder, then fiddled with his collar. "Keeping us from having to incapacitate any more humans tonight."

She rolled her eyes and sat back, her eyes continuing to

flick to the side mirror where it looked like the second officer had lit a cigarette.

Gimme.

Brigid stared at the glowing tip of the cigarette, the fire that lived under her skin pricking her to act; she pushed it back with practiced resolve.

Not tonight. Not here.

The human officer approached Carwyn's window, and the scent of his blood made Brigid's mouth water. She needed to feed, and not the blood in the drug-laced veins of the humans in the back of the van. This one smelled like he believed in clean living, mother's cooking, and wild game.

Delicious.

The police officer finally sauntered to the window. He was a human in his early forties if Brigid was guessing correctly. He looked tired and a little worn-out.

Putting in the hours. Brigid recognized the expression. Punching the clock. This officer was sick of night shifts and bored to tears.

He cleared his throat and spoke in a broad Southern accent. "Evening, sir. Do you happen to know how fast you were going?"

It was as if her husband turned into a pile of friendly Jell-O instead of the mountain of muscle he was. "Oh, I'm so sorry, Officer!" The Welsh vampire laid on a thick Irish accent.

Brigid snorted and covered her mouth, turning it into a cough.

Carwyn continued, "I do believe I was going eighty kilometers an hour, was I not?"

The officer frowned. "'Scuse me? Where y'all from?"

"Oh shur, we're from a humble Catholic mission in Ireland. I'm Father Cormac, and this is Sister Mary Clarence from the Sisterhood of the First Miracle in Kerry." He motioned toward her. "Sister Mary Clarence, wave hello to the nice Garda." Carwyn turned back to the officer. "She can't speak, sir, as she's recently taken a vow of *complete silence.*"

Jesus, Mary, Joseph, and the wee donkey, she was going to kill him when this was over. Brigid leaned forward and waved.

The human frowned. "From... Did you say Ireland?"

"We're borrowing a vehicle from the parish in Los *Angeleez*, where we flew in from our last mission in..." He glanced at Brigid.

She smiled and pointed to her mouth.

"Fiji," Carwyn blurted. "We were on a mission to Fiji."

The police officer was already turned in circles from the accent. "I... I don't know where that is."

"Beautiful place." Carwyn nodded solemnly, his accent growing broader by the moment. "A beautiful part of the Lord's creation and full of heathen... cats."

She snorted again and covered it with another cough.

"Cats?" the officer asked.

"Yes, that's where we work, you see. In animal evangelism." A beatific smile spread over his face. "Working among the world's most vulnerable creatures to show the love of God to the voiceless." He nodded toward Brigid. "That's why my dear sister doesn't speak."

"Because of the cats?"

"Exactly. You don't eat the flesh of God's created animals, do you, young man? Ours is a strictly vegetarian mission."

The officer rallied. "Sir, can I see your driver's license? You were speeding."

"Was I? Surely not." Carwyn fumbled for his wallet. "The sign said fifty-five miles an hour there, and that's nearly ninety kilometers and I was doing only eighty."

The officer frowned. "Right. You were doing eighty in a fifty-five."

"But eighty is below ninety, so I don't see how I could be speeding."

Brigid could see the police officer doing the math in his head.

"I don't... I'm not sure what you're used to—"

"I'm a law-abiding man, sir. A servant of God and the church."

Brigid's skin prickled when one of the humans in the back shifted his arm. The windows might be curtained, but all the officer would have to do was look back and the three bloody and crumpled men would be visible.

Carwyn said, "We're trying to reach our new mission in New Orleans, you see. There's a pack of feral dogs roaming the city that needs to know the Lord. Are you a Christian man, Officer?"

The man stammered. "Of course I am. I mean... I guess it's been a while—"

"Perhaps the Lord brought you to me and my dear Sister Mary Clarence tonight. Do you need to unburden your heart? Perhaps call your mother or grandmother? I have a mobile phone here and we can do that. Can I pray for you, Officer...? I'm sorry, what is your name, sir? We could say a prayer right now. Together."

"Okay, just slow down." The police officer let out a nervous laugh and patted the side of the vehicle. "There's your... blessing. Okay?" He stepped away. "Y'all keep it below fifty-five, you'll make it to New Orleans nice and safe. Take the warning; keep it slow."

Go. Just go now. Brigid braced for another round of blarney from her mate. Carwyn had a tendency to push a bit too far, which often caused more problems than it solved.

"Oh bless you, young man." Carwyn made his voice creak just a little even though the officer looked older than the vampire did. "Bless you and your cats, sir."

"Right. Y'all have a good night and keep it slow."

Carwyn started the van and pulled onto the road, leaving the still-flashing blue lights in the distance behind them.

"Can we turn back to the interstate now?" Brigid asked.

"As soon as we drop off our young friends here." Carwyn glanced across to her. "I see that you've chosen to break your vow of silence."

"Mary Clarence? We're making *Sister Act* jokes to the humans now?"

"Sister Mary Clarence had the voice of an angel; it was a compliment."

"Evangelizing feral cats in Fiji," she muttered. "I can't believe that worked."

"It wasn't the feral cats, darling girl. I threatened to call his mother and pray with him. I could see the Catholic guilt radiating from him as soon as I called myself Father Cormac."

"Never underestimate Catholic guilt." She saw a sign flash by. "Take the next right." She glanced at the human who'd moved before. "They're starting to wake up."

―――――――

ALL VAMPIRES HAD AN ELEMENT GIVEN TO THEM BY their amnis, the immortal energy that lived within them like a current beneath their skin. Her husband was animated by the earth, the foundation of his energy, his immortality, and his massive strength. He stood over six feet with shoulders the size of a minor mountain range, a shock of dark red hair on his head, and a short beard he'd been growing for over a year.

So it came as no surprise to her that in addition to the handcuffs she'd used to secure the men to the railing, Carwyn had also buried them up to their waists in front of the sheriff's substation in Lafayette Parish.

They were definitely not wiggling out of that restraint.

The men all had signs around their necks that advertised their crimes. One read: ASK ME ABOUT THE STOLEN PROPERTY IN MY GARAGE! Another read: I STOLE THE BENSONS' CAR AND BEAT UP AN OLD MAN. And the last one had a sign that read: I DEAL DRUGS TO HIGH SCHOOL STUDENTS.

Carwyn clapped his hands together. "And that's what happens when you try to carjack a couple of vampires."

Brigid saw the moment the humans began to wake.

They were bruised and had to be aching, but she didn't have any sympathy. They'd attempted to disarm her husband with friendly banter and a false welcome at their local pub before sticking a gun to his back in the hallway, forcing him to their van, and trying to rob him.

"Hello, boys." Brigid crouched down in front of the three men. "Remember what happened?"

What happened had been Brigid. The men didn't know that she'd followed them out and saw them pull the firearm. Unlike most vampires, Brigid knew what kind of damage a gun could cause to their kind if used in the right way.

No gun was going to end a vampire's life unless it completely severed their spine at the base of their neck, but a bullet wound anywhere along their nervous system could be catastrophic, if not life-threatening. As best as Brigid could figure, amnis worked with the nervous system, so any major damage to the spine or a primary nerve could produce severe consequences.

She looked at the men. "You put a gun to my husband; that wasn't wise."

The ringleader of the group blinked slowly. "You have fangs."

"I do, but don't flatter yourself. I'd sooner drink from a sewer than your neck. I understand addiction—heroin was my candy—but that doesn't excuse the violence. Get help before you end up dead." She stuffed the number of a local rehab place in the pocket of one of the men. "You don't want to meet me again."

He was still staring. "You have fangs."

"Jaysus." She stood and sighed. "What else should we do? Just leave them here?"

Carwyn was squinting at the darkness. "I think that's our

only option. Do you think the alligators leave the bayou and go roaming?"

"Carwyn, if I have to deal with you chasing any more wildlife—"

"They wouldn't come and take a bite out of one of these two, would they?"

Brigid started to protest the men were fine, but she had to admit Carwyn might have a point. She crouched down in front of another of the men. "Wake up." She patted his cheek, giving him a slight shock from her amnis when he was slow to rouse.

"Fuck." The man jerked awake. "Where the hell am I?"

"How far can an alligator travel from water?" Brigid asked. "We're not from around here, so I don't know."

The man looked around himself in a panic. "George? Buddy?"

"Answer the question." She patted his cheek. "Alligators. Are you in danger from them if we leave you here?"

The man they called Buddy appeared to still be sleeping, but he spoke slowly and in an accent that Brigid barely understood.

"Yeah, gators gonna be a problem all right," he muttered quietly.

Did she care?

Not really, but Carwyn might.

Brigid stood and walked back to the van. "He said the alligators wouldn't be a problem."

Her husband frowned. "Are you sure?"

"Very sure. Come on now; we need to get to New Orleans before sunrise." She walked quickly to the van.

Carwyn started to follow her. "We'll call and report them from the highway."

"Excellent idea." That should get the men arrested before the creatures ate them.

The last thing Brigid needed was another black mark against her soul. She might be immortal, but eventually she'd be judged.

And if it wasn't Saint Peter, she'd have to face Carwyn.

They were heading back toward the highway within minutes, and Brigid sighed in relief. No more local police officers. No more shady characters at darkened petrol stations. They were back in the world of the American interstate system, replete with garish neon signs, brightly lit parking lots the size of football fields, and plastic-packaged food that smelled of chemicals.

"I need to feed." She'd been half hoping the police officer wouldn't fall for Carwyn's friendly-Irish-priest bit and would cause them problems.

No.

He hadn't agreed to be her dinner.

"We'll be at a safe club in two and a half hours. Can you make it that long?"

She cracked open a bottle of blood-wine and drank. "This should keep me from any road rage incidents."

"Good, but crawl in back to drink that unless you want another encounter with law enforcement."

"Fine." She crawled in the back of the van and kicked her feet up on the bench. "Onward then."

"To the wedding!" Carwyn grinned as he took the on-ramp.

"To the wedding." Brigid took an extra gulp of blood-wine.

To the wedding.

The *wedding*.

On second thought, maybe she should have stayed behind with the alligators.

———

Do you get the Elizabeth Hunter newsletter?
For all the latest news about books, extra features, special sales, and exclusive giveaways, subscribe now!

Looking for more?

Whether you're a fan of contemporary fantasy, fantasy romance, or paranormal women's fiction, Elizabeth Hunter has a series for you.

THE ELEMENTAL MYSTERIES

Discover the series that has millions of vampire fans raving! Immortal book dealer Giovanni Vecchio thought he'd left the bloody world of vampire politics behind when he retired as an assassin, but a chance meeting at a university pulls student librarian Beatrice De Novo into his orbit. Now temptation lurks behind every dark corner as Vecchio's growing attachment to Beatrice competes with a series of clues that could lead to a library lost in time, and a powerful secret that could reshape the immortal world.

Ebook/Audiobook/Paperback

Looking for more?

The Cambio Springs Mysteries

Welcome to the desert town of Cambio Springs where the water is cool, the summers sizzle, and all the residents wear fur, feathers, or snakeskin on full moon nights. In a world of cookie-cutter shifter romance, discover a series that has reviewers raving. Five friends find themselves at a crossroads in life; will the tangled ties of community and shared secrets be their salvation or their end?

Ebook/Audiobook/Paperback

The Irin Chronicles

"A brilliant and addictive romantic fantasy series." Hidden at the crossroads of the world, an ancient race battles to protect humanity, even as it dies from within. A photojournalist tumbles into a world of supernatural guardians protecting humanity from the predatory sons of fallen angels, but will Ava and Malachi's attraction to each other be their salvation or their undoing?

Ebook/Audiobook/Paperback

Glimmer Lake

Delightfully different paranormal women's fiction! Robin, Val, and Monica were average forty-something moms when a sudden accident leaves all three of them with psychic abilities they never could have predicted! Now all three are seeing things that belong in a fantasy novel, not their small mountain town. Ghosts, visions, omens of doom. These friends need to stick together if they're going to solve the mystery at the heart of Glimmer Lake.

Ebook/Audiobook/Paperback

And there's more! Please visit ElizabethHunterWrites.com to sign up for her newsletter or read more about her work.

About the Author

ELIZABETH HUNTER is a ten-time *USA Today* and international best-selling author of romance, contemporary fantasy, and paranormal mystery. Based in Central California and Addis Ababa, Ethiopia, she travels extensively to write fantasy fiction exploring world mythologies, history, and the universal bonds of love, friendship, and family. She has published over forty works of fiction and sold over a million books worldwide. She is the author of the Glimmer Lake series, Love Stories on 7th and Main, the Elemental Legacy series, the Irin Chronicles, the Cambio Springs Mysteries, and other works of fiction.

ELIZABETHHUNTERWRITES.COM

About the Author

Also by Elizabeth Hunter

Obsidian's Edge (anthology)

Midnight Labyrinth

Blood Apprentice

The Devil and the Dancer

Night's Reckoning

Dawn Caravan

The Bone Scroll

Pearl Sky

The Elemental Covenant

Saint's Passage

Martyr's Promise

Paladin's Kiss

Bishop's Flight

(Summer 2023)

The Irin Chronicles

The Scribe

The Singer

The Secret

The Staff and the Blade

The Silent

The Storm

The Seeker

Made in the USA
Middletown, DE
26 October 2018